TINO and the TYPHOON

By Alice Geer Kelsey

Illustrated by Isami Kashiwagi

Cover design by Tina DeKam

Cover illustration by Nada Serafimovic

Originally published in 1958

This unabridged edition has updated grammar and spelling.

© 2020 Jenny Phillips

goodandbeautiful.com

Table of Contents

Chapter 1

VALENTINO'S SECRET

Valentino did not call it hiding. He would have said he just happened to be polishing the red outboard motor when his father, Lighthouse Keeper Rodolfo Luna, needed someone to climb the ladder. Its thirty-one dizzy rungs marched up outside the slim white lighthouse in the center of the Philippine coastal village of Darapidap. Its beacon signaled, "This way home," to fishermen in their narrow outrigger *bangkas* far out in the South China Sea.

It was not his fault, Valentino would have said, that the five-horsepower motor he was shining happened to be where his father could not see it, or see him as he polished. It was the lighthouse keeper himself, not Valentino, who was careful to store it in the thatched bamboo shed with the motors of neighbor fishermen whose wooden *bangkas* were drawn up on the sandy beach waiting till time and weather for night fishing.

Valentino heard his father call amiably, "I left the empty kerosene tin in the balcony beside the lamp. I need it. Who will be the one to go up for it?"

The boy was glad there were no windows in the bamboo shed. He squatted behind the door, hidden from the doorway. He knew what would come next.

"Tino! Tino!" his father called less pleasantly. "Where is that Valentino?"

"He is somewhere around," said Tino's mother. She was sitting on her heels beside the shallow laundry tub near the pump on their high back porch. "I saw him a minute ago."

The boy knew what he hoped to hear next. And he heard it.

"I will be the one to climb the ladder, Tatang!" It was the cheerful voice of his younger sister, Erlinda. For the hundredth time, Tino was grateful that she sensed his shameful secret and came to his rescue.

"Your lazy brother should be the one." Tino could feel the frown on his father's rugged, weather-lined face. "He is never around when someone must climb the lighthouse ladder."

"Oh, I like to climb it!" Erlinda's brisk voice came from the foot of the ladder—then from higher—and higher. "Tino is not lazy. He is just—just—" Tino wondered what she would say. Would she give away his humiliating secret? He was relieved when she finished, "Tino is just busy doing other things."

"I am going up, too!" Tino heard his brother Pedro say. He was four years younger than Tino. Everybody called him Pedring.

"Me—up—too!" lisped Rosario. She was between Pedring and Baby Pepito in age. "Me—up—too!"

Danger to his little sister brought Tino running from the bamboo shed. He dashed across the hard-packed dirt yard to grab little Rosario as she took a fumbling step from first to second ladder rung. He could not explain why he gave her a spiteful little shake as he set her on the ground. He was angry with someone, but not with her—nor with Pedring—nor with his adored father—nor with loyal Erlinda.

Holding Rosario's small hand firmly, he looked up in time to see Pedring climb the last rungs and join Erlinda on the balcony encircling the big pressure lamp that burned faithfully every night from dusk to dawn. Tino watched his brother and sister walk around the balcony to view their world from above. Everything they could see was familiar to him, but he wondered how it all looked from so high in the air.

First, he saw them look across the white beach with its colorful moored *bangkas* to the rippling South China Sea, blue and empty to the horizon except for a few hovering gulls. Erlinda and Pedring might possibly see a school of porpoises leaping from the water or perhaps the lone boat of a fisherman. There would be no ocean-going ships in sight. The big ships always sailed far from shore to round the northern arm of Lingayen Gulf.

Next, Tino watched Erlinda and Pedring look down at their own small *barrio*—a village mostly of bamboo huts with roofs thatched with cogon grass or nipa palm. They would also be seeing the few wooden houses, their church with its four open sides, and their frame schoolhouse flying its Philippine flag. Perhaps some of the houses were hidden by the graceful coconut palms whose crowns of huge leaves towered above them. Tino heard the trot and rattle of a two-wheeled, horse-drawn wooden *calesa*. He wondered if the small horse and carriage would be hidden by the rows of fine-leaved camachile trees growing on either side of the dirt road connecting Darapidap with the distant highway to the east and with the bigger *barrio* across the river to the north.

Then, Tino saw his brother and sister look east, away from the sea, over the wet green rice fields where the few farmers of their *barrio* worked with their heavy-footed gray water buffalo called carabao. The river twisted slowly through those fields after rushing down from the forested hills to lose its brown water in the ever-moving, blue-green sea. Tino thought he would like to see that whole river in one piece, not from curve to curve as he always saw it.

The far view would be fun, but not worth the price of climbing to any dizzy height.

Now, Erlinda and Pedring were looking north where the river emptied into the sea. Tino could imagine the busy life they were watching. They would see Cesar poling his ferry *bangka* across the stream, *barrio* friends dragging their nets for *bangús* fry, old women squatting at the river's edge to talk together, a few fishermen standing waist-deep to throw and pull their round dragnets in the lively water at the river's mouth, and children playing their sand games in the wide spaces of the beach. They could see across the river the neighboring *barrio* where more people lived and some houses were bigger.

Trying to think how the familiar scenes would look from the balcony of the lighthouse made Tino's head buzz and his stomach flutter. His legs felt as limp as the macaroni-like rice *pancit* noodles his mother cooked for special occasions.

The few times he had been forced to make the climb, he had not looked down, had not looked around. He had done his work and come back to solid ground as soon as he could, eyes up all the time. It was a year since he had gone up the ladder. He remembered, for school had started in June after the long vacation of the dry season. Since then he had learned to delay till someone else started up; he was handy at being out of sight, as he was today, when his father called,

"Someone must climb the lighthouse ladder."

Valentino intended to avoid climbing that ladder for the rest of his life. He would not scale it again if he lived to be as old as Tata Picoy, who no longer went out with the fishing *bangkas* but cast his throw-net near shore or talked with anyone who had time to listen to his wisdom and his stories.

Tino watched Erlinda and Pedring scramble down the ladder carrying the empty kerosene tin. He knew he could thank Erlinda that he had not been compelled to mount the tower recently. The brother and sister, so different from each other, had an unspoken agreement. Erlinda understood Tino's fear of high places and was quick to climb for him. Tino, on the other hand, understood that his brave little tomboy of a sister had no more mechanical sense than the black pig that rooted contentedly in their yard and slept under their high-perched hut. For Erlinda, the long wooden pump handle balked, the stone grindstone stuck, the lamp wick gave a sputtering flicker, the hook of the woven bamboo shutters would not fit, and a knife was a thing of danger. Tino found plenty of ways to thank Erlinda for taking the high places for him.

As Erlinda and Pedring reached ground, Tino felt his handsome father, usually so jolly, staring unsmiling at him from the doorway of their bamboo and cogon house. The boy knew from his father's disapproving look that it would be uncomfortable to let the lighthouse keeper speak first.

"Oh, Tatang!" said Tino. "You should see how our outboard motor shines! I am the one who has polished it. Ours is older than the motors of Tomas or Gabriel or Bonifacio. But it looks newest of all. It is so clean! It is so rubbed!"

Rodolfo Luna stared in grim silence. Tino felt like crawling back into the shed, but he prattled on, "Shall I oil the motor now? And grease it?"

There was no answer. "I know everything about outboard motors," Tino chattered. "I know how to fit them in the *bangkas*—how to pour in the gasoline— how to start them going. I have watched you and Gabriel and Bonifacio till I know everything. Tatang, when may I run the outboard motor in our *bangka*?"

This time Tino's father had an answer. In a voice low with displeasure, Tatang said, "My son, you are not old enough to run the outboard motor."

"I am as old as Rafael. I am older than Vicente. They both run *bangka* motors. Rafael goes out fishing at night." Tino could hear his mother's gasp of surprise to hear her son doing what no Filipino boy should do: arguing with his father. Tino tried to avoid his father's eyes, but he could feel disapproval floating about him like a thick fog. He squared his shoulders and said, "I am old enough, no?"

"You will be old enough—" Tatang waited till Tino

looked him in the eye. "You will be old enough to run the outboard motor in our *Sea Gull* when you are old enough to climb the lighthouse ladder instead of hiding when someone must go up."

Tino had no answer. He stood looking at the lighthouse that rose so slim and white. Though small compared to the beacons that guided ocean-going ships, it towered above the little houses where the fishermen neighbors lived, above the camachile trees that shaded the rough road, above the tallest coconut palms of Darapidap or of Tomurong across the river.

Valentino stood still, counting the iron rungs of the ladder, though he already knew their number: "One—two—three—" up to "twenty-nine—thirty— thirty-one." His knees felt shaky as he turned back into the bamboo shed to find comfort in polishing his love, the red outboard motor of the *Sea Gull*, their graceful gray and white *bangka* moored on the beach.

Chapter 2

THE FLAG ON THE CALESA

The Luna family took the shrill crowing of their
long-legged rooster as a command. The mother was
first to sit up on her sleeping mat of woven *buri* palm.
Though the *sawali* windows of crisscross bamboo
strips had been closed for the night, the house had
plenty of chinks through which the dim light could
announce the sky's change from gray to pink.

The night noises were over—the lonely hoot of the
owl, the "cheep-cheep" of crickets, the monotonous
"took-took" of the bird called the nightjar, the stirring
of bats' wings in the papaya tree. There were only the
sounds common to both day and night—the sweet
humming of locusts, the "chuck-chuck" of little lizards
chasing insects on the walls, the waking songs of
many birds.

Soon the mother had the fire of driftwood and dried palm stalks burning between the three stones on their slab in the kitchen lean-to.

The smell from frying rice and fish made the three older children sit up on their mats and stretch away the sleep. Their father, tired from night fishing, slept on. So did little Rosario and Baby Pepito. These two small ones were not faced with hard work to do before school began at half past seven.

The children stepped lightly on the cool, flexible floor of split bamboo. They knew Tatang would be jollier if he finished his sleep. They dressed in their wading clothes and washed under the pump on the back porch. They rolled up their mats to pile with the small hard pillows in a corner of the one bedroom.

"Good morning, Nanang!" they greeted their pretty mother as they walked through the *sala* into the kitchen. Like so many Filipina women, she was graceful and young-looking in spite of a big family that kept her busy.

They ate silently. There was little to say so early in the morning. The four plates were washed in cold water and left to drain and sun on the outdoor shelf of the kitchen window.

Nanang and the three older children went down the five steps of the bamboo ladder. Under their house they picked up a big net of fine mesh, a large white clam shell, a white pan, a tin tub, and a big pottery jar.

Balancing these on their heads, they walked barefoot down the rutted dirt road that connected their *barrio* with the one across the river. The children preferred to run along the beach with the waves cooling their toes, but with work to do before school, they took the shorter way.

"I hope we are first at the river today," said Valentino.

"Not first!" Erlinda pointed at fresh footprints in the road. "A man—a woman—a child—a smaller child—a dog."

Reaching the slow-flowing brown river, they found themselves the second family to start netting for the tiny fry of the fish called *bangús* or milkfish. Even Cesar the ferryman had not yet come down to his *bangka*, whose frequent trips linked their *barrio* with its neighbors across the river.

"Tino and I will drag the net first," said Nanang. "Pedring, you carry the pan. Erlinda, you wait with the tub and jar. We must do as much work as we can before you have to leave for school."

"I would like to stay here working with you, Nanang," Erlinda offered cheerfully.

"I want to go to school," said Valentino.

"Why?" Pedring stared at his big brother. Who would sit at a desk memorizing from books when he could be out in the fresh breezes of the South China Sea?

They waded waist deep against the incoming tide.

"When I finish my lessons early," Tino explained, "Miss Ventura lets me look at books about machines and engines and motors."

"Well, there is no machine for dragging the river!" Nanang picked up one side of the fine-meshed net and motioned for Tino to take the other side. Together they stepped into the water and waded waist deep against the incoming tide toward the mouth of the stream. Pedring walked beside them on the river's bank carrying the white basin.

At Nanang's signal, Pedring waded out to hand her the small white pan. Tino and his mother lifted the net and held it higher till its contents were in a small space resting near the surface. With the basin, Nanang skillfully scooped all that was left in the net.

"Let me carry it back to Erlinda," offered Pedring.

"Careful! Do not spill!" Nanang warned.

Pedring walked sure-footed in the warm, hard sand. He cherished the pan as though it held jewels. He knew that those tiny hairlike wrigglers in the water in his pan could each grow to be a delicious big *bangús*, a favorite fish of Filipinos.

Erlinda knew what to do next. As soon as Pedring set the white pan beside her, she began skimming its water with her white clam shell to take out tiny fish, scraps of sticks or leaves, shreds of seaweed— everything but the salt water and the almost invisible baby *bangús* fish. These seemed like tiny hairs, a quarter-of-an-inch long, swimming in the water. After she had cleaned out all the rubbish, Erlinda gently dumped water and fry in the big tub and began skimming again with her clam shell, transferring the tiny swimming fish into the pottery jar.

"What a big jar to fill with such tiny wriggling things!" said Erlinda.

"But three *pesos* is a lot of money when we get the jar full," Nanang reminded her.

"Did the man who buys them tell the truth?" asked Valentino. "Are there really 3,000 *bangús* fry in one of these jars?"

"I have never counted," admitted Nanang. "The buyers say they count once in a while, to be sure we are not selling them more water and less *bangús* fry."

"I would like to see the fish ponds where these wrigglers grow to be fish," said Tino.

"Someday you will travel," Nanang promised. "Someday we will take a holiday and ride on the bus to see our beautiful country."

"I would sit on the front seat beside the driver," dreamed Tino. "I would watch everything he did. I would learn how he made the bus start—and turn— and speed—and stop."

Nanang laughed. "After the first five kilometers you would be offering to drive the bus. Well, as I said before, there is no machine for netting *bangús* fry. To work!"

So again Tino and his mother waded toward the incoming tide, dragging the net between them. Nanang's skirt hung wet to her waist. Tino's clothes were brown with river water. The warm winds flapped their net. Back and forth they went, time after time. Always, Pedring carried the white basin full of water and wrigglers back to Erlinda who skimmed and poured and skimmed again. Slowly the water line in the big pottery jar rose.

Other families came to the river to drag their nets and fill their jars for the owners of fish ponds. Cesar poled his ferry *bangka* back and forth across the river. Three horse-drawn *calesas* were on hand to carry people through the *barrio* to the big town on the highway. It always amazed Tino how many people could climb over the high wooden wheels and squeeze into the two seats of one of the small square-roofed carriages.

"See the *calesa* with a Philippine flag?" called Pedring. "Why? Is this a special day?"

"What day of the month is this?" Nanang wondered as she looked at the red and blue flag with its yellow sun and stars on a field of white. Then she remembered. "This is the third of July. The *calesa* driver is getting ready to celebrate Philippine Independence Day tomorrow. July 4, 1946, was the day the United States of America gave us our independence."

"Was that what the war was about—the war when you and Tatang and the other people from our *barrio* had to live in the mountains?" Pedring asked. "Did we beat the United States in that war?"

"Oh Pedring, Pedring! What a question!" Nanang stared at her second son. "Have we let you grow so big knowing so little about your country? The Americans *gave* us our independence. They wanted us to be free. We did not need to fight for freedom from them. American and Filipino soldiers fought shoulder to shoulder in the Great War. They walked side by side in the Death March of Bataan. They starved together in prison camps. The Americans kept on helping us after we were independent and had our own Republic of the Philippines. Americans and Filipinos are friends."

"Then what was that war?" asked Pedring. "I mean that war when everyone went to the mountains. Why did you go, Nanang? What did you do there?"

Nanang looked at the sun to see how far it had risen above the horizon. "Time to go home and clean up for school now," she said. "But I make you a promise. We will take time off from work tomorrow, our Independence Day, to answer your questions. You three run now. I will wait here by the jar of *bangús* fry till your Tatang comes to pull the net with me. Remind him the tide is still coming in. Tell him to leave Rosario and Pepito with Tita Gloria."

The children started along the road toward home. They would not have walked so calmly if they had known what their mother was planning as she waited by the edge of the river. They would not have sat in school so quietly if they had dreamed what she was saying to their father and what he was answering. They would not have played with their friends on the way home from school if they had guessed what they would hear when they sat down to their noon meal of freshly cooked rice, little boiled crabs, and sweet-potato greens.

"Tomorrow is a holiday," Tatang announced as they ate together. "Tomorrow we will take a trip to celebrate the independence of our young Republic of the Philippines. We will have a picnic on the mountains where your nanang and I lived with our families during War and Occupation."

Tatang looked at his children with his broad holiday smile. They were as surprised as he expected them to be. He was pleased with his plan, as though he had thought it up himself. And Nanang, smiling at them all, was glad that Tatang had taken the plan as his own.

"But it is very far away, no?" said Erlinda.

"It is far," agreed Tatang, "but a bus can carry us there and back in a day."

"A bus?" Valentino hopped up and started turning an imaginary steering wheel as he made the house sway with his prancing.

"We will take a *calesa* to the highway, the first *calesa* in the morning," Tatang told his smiling children. "Then we will take the bus to the mountain pass near the sea. Your uncle will go with us. Tito Manuel knows the way into our hiding place in the mountains even better than I do. You remember, he was a guerrilla captain when we fled there from our village."

"Will Tita Gloria come with us?" Erlinda always wanted others to share her good times.

"Your aunt is too lame. It is hard for her to get in and out of the bus," said Nanang. "She will take care of Rosario and Pepito so I can go with you."

Erlinda snuggled against her mother. "I am glad you will go with us."

"You will show us where you lived in the mountains," said Pedring.

"You will tell us what happened there," said Valentino.

Tatang and Nanang nodded. "That will be our Independence Day celebration!" said Tatang.

Chapter 3

THE FOURTH OF JULY

On the morning of July fourth, it was hard to tell whether the black and red rooster woke the Lunas or they woke the rooster. "In—de—pen—dence *Da—ay!*" Tino sang to the tune of the cock's crowing.

"Sh!" His mother reminded him of neighbors whose thin bamboo or nipa walls were not far from their own. "Sleep a little more. If we start now, there will be a long wait for a *calesa.*"

"Oh, I took care of that!" Tino laughed as he rolled up his *buri* sleeping mat. "I told the father of Salvador we would need a *calesa* very early this morning."

"How early?" Tatang's question came through a waking yawn.

Tino lighted the small kerosene flare before he answered. "I told him we were going on the first *calesa*. He counted how many fares we would be. Then he said, 'I will be the one whose *calesa* will make the first trip.'"

Tino's next words came from the kitchen lean-to where he was laying driftwood between the three stones of the fireplace. "I am making a good breakfast fire for you, Nanang."

The cock crowed again, and Tino sang with it, "In—de—pen—dence *Da—ay*!"

Erlinda and Pedring sat up on their *buri* mats and joined the chant, "In—de—pen—dence *Da—ay*!"

"Sh!" Nanang pointed at Rosario and Baby Pepito. "Oh, please do not waken them. Your Tita Gloria will take care of our babies today. We must not leave them sleepy and cross for her."

The three-room house quivered on its six strong posts as the family hurried to make ready for their holiday. Trips were a rare experience. Each move of preparation was new and thrilling. They must eat a bigger breakfast so they would not be hungry on the bus. They must decide what clothes would be good enough for the bus ride but not too good for the hike and picnic in the mountains. They must wrap cold rice, chicken, boiled shrimps, and green papaya pickles in clean banana leaves for lunch. There was the small black pig to be tied securely by one leg to a house post with plenty of food and water within reach. There was the walk across the hard-packed dirt yard to see that Tito Manuel had eaten breakfast and that Tita Gloria was ready to care for Rosario and Pepito. They must remind Gabriel to light the big pressure lamp in the lighthouse if they were delayed till nearly dark. They must take their palm-leaf raincapes and their big bowl-shaped hats to be ready for any weather. It was the rainy season, when clear morning sky was often followed by a tropical downpour.

They had reached the point where Nanang was saying, "Have we forgotten anything?" when they heard the rattle of *calesa* wheels and the clip of small horse hoofs on the road in front of the house.

"The *tatang* of Salvador is here!" Tino's voice was full of pride. After all, he was the one who brought the *calesa* so early.

"And Salvador is with him!" came a boy's voice from the driver's seat of the two-wheeled wooden cart painted a cheery red and blue. "I have lunch and bus fare. I am going with you."

To make room for six more passengers, the driver slid from his seat to the narrow ridge close to the horse's tail. The Lunas loaded their lunch baskets and raincapes into the *calesa*. Tino, Erlinda, and Pedring scrambled over one high wooden wheel and squeezed into the driver's seat with Salvador. Nanang, Tatang, and tall Tito Manuel climbed over the other wheel and settled in the seat for passengers.

The *calesa* driver jerked the reins of good manila rope as he said, "I give you all a free ride to the National Road. You give Salvador a holiday." He beamed at them all, and they smiled just as happily. "I want my boy to see where we hid during the War and Occupation. I want him to hear the story from Manuel, the hero of Darapidap."

Nobody doubted Salvador's welcome. It was the way of the *barrio,* for neighbors to help one another. They were used to sharing both good times and bad times.

Tino, who was quick in arithmetic, multiplied the fifteen-*centavo* fare by six and found their saving lacked only ten *centavos* of being a *peso.* He multiplied the ninety *centavos* by two when Salvador's father said, "I will try to be at the National Road when you come back this afternoon. If I am not there, wait for me. I will come after I deliver my load."

One *peso* and eighty *centavos* saved, and his friend Salvador to share the day's fun! Pedring and Erlinda were good companions, but Salvador was Tino's own age. Tino was glad he had thought to tell Salvador's father about their holiday plan.

With a Philippine flag flying from each corner of its wooden top, the *calesa* went rattling down the uneven road. The little horse trotted rapidly when the road was fairly level. He slowed to a mincing walk when the holes in the road made the *calesa* lurch and roll as though it would turn over or collapse.

"I am glad you fly flags on Independence Day," Tito Manuel praised the driver. Because Manuel was *barrio* lieutenant, his approval was valued. Then he leaned toward the children and asked, "Who can tell us what the flag means?"

"The yellow sun is for our great Republic of the Philippines," Tino quoted what he had learned in school.

"The three yellow stars are for the three parts of that Republic," Erlinda recited in her schoolroom voice. "Luzon, Mindanao, and the Visayans."

"Good!" Tito Manuel approved. "And what do the colors mean?"

The four children on the front seat answered in chorus, "Red is for courage. Blue is for truth. White is for purity."

Tito Manuel clapped his approval. "What a fine thing schools are to teach about your country!"

"Schools are best on holidays like this," said Pedring, "or in the dry season when we have the long vacation."

The *calesa* rolled between the rows of low green camachile trees and the scattered small houses of planks or bamboo with roofs of thatch or corrugated iron. Some of the *barrio* friends were sleeping late because of the holiday. Others were leaning out their windows to wave the family off on its trip.

News had spread fast that the father of Salvador was making an early trip to the National Road to carry the Lunas and their Tito Manuel on a holiday. Wives were wishing their own husbands had such good ideas. Boys were wishing their own fathers were *calesa* drivers so they might have had a chance at the holiday trip.

Many of the grownups were remembering the days when they had fled to the mountains. They were wondering if they would really like to see those places of adventure and danger again. Or would they rather forget it all? It was good to celebrate the day thinking with pride of the independence of their young country.

The *calesa* turned away from the sea and rattled past the schoolhouse. The doors were locked for the holiday.

"No flag!" Erlinda pointed at the tall, empty flagpole. "The Philippine flag should fly on our Independence Day."

"Many flags will fly today," said Tatang. "The school flag will fly again after the holiday, as it does every school day."

The thought of that flag raising started Salvador whistling the marching tune of the "Philippine National Anthem." Soon they were all singing it together. Most of them sang in their own dialect, but Salvador and Tino tried out the English words they had learned in school.

Land of the morn - ing, Child of the sun re - turn - ing
Land dear and ho - ly, Cradle of no - ble he - roes,

With fer - vor burn - ing, Thee do our souls a - dore.
Ne'er shall in - va - ders Tram - ple thy sa - cred shore.

The *calesa* clattered along the rutted road between damp green rice fields. It dodged a fuzzy gray baby carabao that had wandered from its grazing mother's side into the quiet road. Everything was clean and dew fresh in the early dawn light. A pair of small brown rice birds, called mannikins, rose from a field and settled on the broad backs of two carabaos shining with fresh mud.

"Why do birds ride on backs of carabao?" asked Pedring. "If I were a carabao, I would poke them off with my big tough horns or switch them off with my hard ropy tail."

"The birds are eating the insects that bother the carabao," Tino explained.

Tatang laughed. "That is a sensible answer, but it is not what Old Pacifico would say. Have you heard him tell why the rice bird rides the carabao?"

The children always liked the stories Old Pacifico told. Usually he was called Tata Picoy: Tata for respect and Picoy, the nickname for Pacifico. They turned toward their father, ready for the story.

"I cannot tell it as well as Old Pacifico. It goes something like this," began Tatang.

"The carabao and the rice bird had a bet one day when they were beside the river. It could have been our own river because it happened near where a stream flowed into the sea. They were betting which one could drink more water. The big carabao naturally said he could drink more than the tiny bird. But strangely, the little brown mannikin said she could drink more than the carabao.

"The bird was choosy about time and place for the contest. The carabao did not care. He met her at the edge of the river just when and where the bird told him to come.

"'You drink first,' the mannikin said politely to the carabao.

"The carabao thanked the bird for giving him the first turn. He waded a few steps into the river and thrust his wide damp nose into the brackish water. He drank and drank and drank. Swish-swish, he sucked till his mud-covered sides stuck out twice their normal size. Then the bird pointed at the river and said, 'Look, there is more water than when you began.'

"'Well, try it yourself.' The carabao could not deny that he was standing in deeper water than when he began to drink. 'See if you can drink enough with your tiny beak to make the river smaller.'

"It took the bird many minutes to get ready to

"Why do birds ride on backs of carabao?"
asked Pedring.

begin. She smoothed her feathers. She fluttered about choosing a place to drink. She flew over many rice fields, inviting her bird relatives to watch the contest. The carabao thought she was wasting time, but a carabao never hurries nor worries. He lay in the mud and waited patiently.

"At last the bird seemed satisfied. She stepped down to the edge of the river and put her beak in the water. Then a most surprising thing happened right in front of the eyes of the carabao, whose stomach was so full of brackish water that it sloshed when he moved.

"Slowly, very slowly, the river began to grow smaller. No one could deny the waterline was going down—and down—and down as the bird stood with her tiny beak in the water. As the line crept lower, little islands appeared where there had been water a few minutes before. A sand bar came into sight, reaching almost across the river. But still, the mannikin stood with her beak in position for drinking. The big, slow carabao was ashamed to be beaten by a little bird.

"'You are better than I am,' the carabao said in his humblest voice.

"'Then I am your master, no?' said the rice bird.

"'From this day you and all your relatives are my masters,' said the poor, shamed carabao.

"'Then let me ride on your back to prove it,' said the little brown mannikin.

"And from that day to this, the rice bird has been master of the carabao and can ride on his broad gray back whenever she pleases," Tatang ended his story.

"Oh, I see what happened!" Pedring guessed the bird's trick. Having lived all his life by a river that grew larger or smaller with incoming and outgoing tides, Pedring could laugh at the carabao with his ignorant inland ways. "The bird made the carabao drink when the tide was coming in and the river was growing higher. Then the bird fluttered around wasting time till the tide was going out before she began to drink."

Erlinda waved her hand at a brown and white bird balancing serenely on the back of an indifferent carabao. "Smart little mannikin!"

The folk tale had taken the time the little horse needed to pull the square *calesa* between the open fields to the first houses and stores of the big town where their *barrio* road met the National Road. The family and Salvador piled out at the store where buses going north stopped for passengers.

A radio inside the store was broadcasting alternate music and weather forecasts. Valentino slipped inside to inspect the radio and ask questions of anyone who would answer. He had fun learning about the radio, but he was not happy to hear it was run by electricity. Darapidap had no electricity. It was no use even to dream about a radio in his bamboo-and-cogon hut.

There was no hope for a radio anywhere in his *barrio*, though it would be such fun to turn those dials and bring sounds from the air!

"Tino! Tino! Where is that Valentino?" called Tatang.

"Here I am!" The boy ran from the store and joined his family.

The *calesa* driver waited with them till some return passengers hailed him for a ride back to the sea.

Soon a big red bus, labeled VIGAN, pulled up beside the store. It looked cozy and jolly with its wooden benches stretched from one open side to the other. There seemed no place for another person when it stopped, but friendly people began to move closer together to make room.

Before his mother could tell him where to go, Tino had squeezed into a six-inch space on the front bench where he could watch the driver at work. The six inches had widened as he settled between a heavy woman carrying a basket of live chickens and a boy who insisted on riding in the outside seat, even if it made the new passengers stumble over his feet. Tito Manuel found a bit of space directly behind them. Tatang held Pedring on his lap in the sixth row. Pedring liked this because it raised him high enough to see over the fluttering head scarves of the women in front of him. He could see his pretty mother take her best red scarf from her bag and tie it around her smooth black hair. He could see Tino asking smiling questions of the other people on the front row till he moved, one place at a time, closer to the driver.

"Good for Tino!" His admiring little brother chuckled as the boy made his last move. Now Tino was sitting next to the driver. He would not miss a single motion.

With much honking of its horn and chattering of its passengers, the bus was on its journey. The children liked to hear the people talk. Most of them spoke their own language, Ilocano. A few were using some of the seventy other dialects spoken in the Philippines.

The National Road curved on and on, sometimes between sea and mountains, sometimes between fields of corn or tobacco, sometimes through small *barrios*. Soon it came to a place where steep and wild mountains came close to the road on both sides.

"Psst!" It was Tito Manuel's signal to stop the bus.

"Psst!" whistled Tatang.

"Psst!" echoed Valentino, Pedring, and Salvador.

"Psst! Psst! Psst!" came from men all over the bus who wanted to help.

The big bus pulled to the side of the road and stopped. Passengers were surprised to watch the family climb out in such a lonely spot. Some turned to stare as the bus drove on, leaving the Lunas and Salvador alone at the side of the highway with their raincapes and baskets. These passengers seemed to be looking for a side road or a mountain *barrio* where this family might be going.

Tino waved goodbye to his new friend, the bus driver, who answered with a special honk of his horn. Then Tino shouldered his share of the load and followed Tito Manuel up a trail so overgrown that only a man who had been a wartime guerrilla would have recognized it as a place to walk.

Chapter 4

GUERRILLA HILLS

Accustomed to the sea and its sandy shores, the children made slow progress in the jungle growth of the mountainside. On the beach at home, they always ran ahead of Tatang and Nanang, and far ahead of Tito Manuel who was older. On the vine-draped trail, to their surprise, it was their parents and uncle who stepped easily over fallen logs that tripped the children, or dodged branches that reached out to scratch and tear, or avoided slippery mud and dead leaves.

"I feel like a girl again!" There was a song in Nanang's voice. "How we used to skip and run over these hills! We knew where the wild papayas were ripe and where the coconuts were ready to pick."

"And where the wild bananas grew the sweetest! And where the wild doves could be snared!" Their father was as excited as Nanang to be back in the hills known so well between 1942 and 1945 when life in their own *barrio* was not safe.

"I remember how you young things used to run around!" said Tito Manuel. "What a hard time you gave to us guerrilla soldiers! How we scolded you and your parents when you wandered from camp into danger!"

"What danger, Tito Manuel?" asked Valentino, dodging branches and slippery spots behind his quick-striding uncle.

"Snakes?" Pedring peered nervously into the rank jungle growth that crowded their narrow trail.

Their father's laugh came from far up the path as he called back, "Much worse than snakes!"

"Getting lost?" Erlinda felt insecure. She was used to the everlasting swash of waves on sandy beaches, saying, "West is this way. West is this way."

Their mother's laugh came from the trail behind them. She had chosen to walk last in case anyone was hurt or tired. "Not much chance of getting lost when we had our dog Brownie to herd us. He was better than the guerrillas to keep us near camp. Besides, in spite of what Tito Manuel says, we were afraid of the real dangers. We did not dare wander far."

"Tell us about those real dangers," Tino asked again.

"While we eat we will tell you," promised Tito Manuel.

After a long climb, they stopped in an open place under coconut palms where there were plenty of green coconuts to provide cool sweet drink. Salvador and Pedring each shinnied up a richly fruiting tree and tossed down heavy young coconuts. Tatang took his *bolo* knife from its sheath at his belt. With a few deft strokes of the *bolo*, he changed each coconut to a big cup of clear coconut water, sweet and refreshing. Meanwhile, Nanang had opened the picnic baskets and was passing out the rolled banana leaves full of good food.

Tito Manuel was too hungry to keep his promise till he had eaten. When his banana leaf was nearly empty, he remembered. "You want to hear about our real dangers when we lived here in the hills."

The children moved closer, the better to listen and ask questions.

"Our greatest danger came from Japanese snipers," he said. "Look around you. See how easy it would be for an enemy with a gun to hide in a bamboo thicket? See how he could keep out of sight behind a vine-draped giant of a jungle tree?"

"But Japanese are nice," protested Erlinda. "We study about them at school. They like flowers, dolls, kites, and poetry. They work hard. They are very clean and tidy. They sent the Filipinos much good stuff called reparations—cement, machinery, railroad cars, building material. Why should they try to shoot you?"

"It was war," said Tatang. "People are not their good selves when there is war. We are glad you are learning to admire the Japanese people. We are glad that you have heard so little about the bitterness and suffering that war brought to the Philippines back in the forties. It is the way of our people to talk about what is happy and forget what is bad."

"It is a good way," murmured Nanang.

"My father said he wanted me to learn about those days from Manuel, the hero of Darapidap," Salvador remembered. "What did he mean?"

"Oh, it was nothing." Tito Manuel took a long drink of fresh coconut water before he explained.

"I happened to be captain of the guerrillas for this area. Enemy soldiers often landed on the beach to our north and tried to go south on the highway. To do that, they had to go through that narrow pass where our bus dropped us off this morning. Our guerrillas managed to wipe them out or turn them back whenever they tried to go through the pass. We saved several towns and *barrios* that way."

"How could you always be there to fire when they went through the pass?" asked Tino. "How did you know when the enemy was coming?"

"Our *bolo* men, or runners, kept us informed," said Tito Manuel. "We had *bolo* men hiding in *garretas*, thatched shacks near every town where there was a Japanese garrison. Each *barrio* had its *garreta* and runners. News of enemy movement was carried from one *garreta* to the next and so on till all our people were warned. They knew when they must move farther up into the hills; the guerrillas knew when and where to attack."

"Was that the way news traveled in all parts of the Philippines?" asked Tino.

"Some guerrillas had an easier way—radio," answered Tito Manuel. "Nearer big towns, the guerrillas on the hills and some loyal people in the towns kept each other informed by radio."

"But how could they?" Tino always tried to figure how things would work. "Radio needs electricity. Guerrillas did not have that in the hills."

"There's a kind of radio that runs on batteries," explained Tito Manuel.

"Batteries?" asked Tino. "What are they?"

"That is a question to ask Miss Ventura when you go to school tomorrow," suggested Nanang. She knew there would be questions none of them could answer if Tino started asking about battery radios. "Your uncle has not told you the real reason he is called the hero of Darapidap. Ask him about the time our *barrio* was almost burned."

"Tell us, Tito Manuel," said the children.

"You do not know?" he asked, surprised.

"We do not talk about those experiences to our children," said Nanang. "We try to forget those days of fear and hate. These are happier times, and we live in them gladly. But still, on our Independence Day, we think our children should know how others suffered and were brave so that we could have the freedom the Americans had promised us."

"I think I know what your father wants me to tell you, Salvador." Tito Manuel's face was grim, remembering days he liked to forget. "It was at a time when some of our people had gone back to their *barrios*, at both Darapidap and Tomurong. They were tired of the hills. They longed for their sea. They wanted to try living in their own homes again. They took their *bangkas* out fishing. At low tide they netted for crabs and lobsters at the coral pools across the river. They cooked the seaweed that washed in on the tide. They cast their dragnets for the tiny silvery fish that are so tasty with rice. It was good to be having food from the sea again.

"One day, three enemy soldiers came into the *barrio*. They asked for food. Our people did not know what they would demand next. They feared their guns."

"Where were you and your guerrillas, Tito Manuel?" Tino asked.

"Up here in the hills. We had no touch with our *barrios* unless a *bolo* man ran from *garreta* to *garreta* carrying news," explained Tito Manuel. "The Japanese soldiers really did not do much harm. No matter what their plans were, they had no time to hurt our *barrios*. You see, our fishermen disposed of them first.

"Before many days, the Japanese officers missed the three soldiers. They knew they had gone to our *barrio*. They knew the soldiers had not returned. More soldiers and officers came to our *barrios*, threatening punishment. They threatened to burn Darapidap and Tomurong till not a house stood—till not a person was alive.

"At night, one of the fishermen ran from the *barrio*, following the dark banks of the river through the blackness of the jungle. He made his way to the nearest shack where a *bolo* man waited to run with news. This *bolo* man ran to us in the hills. He told us what was going to happen to our homes and our families unless we did something to save them."

Tino jumped ahead to guess the ending. "So you led your guerrillas down to the lowlands, Tito Manuel. You drove away the enemy officers and soldiers, no?'

"Not so easy as that," said Tito Manuel. "There were many Japanese soldiers and few of us. They knew all the tricks of jungle fighting as well as we did."

"Then what could you do?" asked Tino.

"I went down to our *barrio* alone to face the Japanese officers and soldiers," said Tito Manuel.

"You were afraid, no?" asked Tino.

"Of course I was afraid," said Tito Manuel. "I remember how I whistled to myself and made my shivering legs march forward to my own whistling when they wanted to run away. When I met the enemy soldiers, I thrust both hands in my pockets to hide their shaking. I expected to be killed, but I had a job to do. And so—God forgive me for saying what was not true—I took all the blame on myself. I said I had ordered my guerrillas to kill the three soldiers. At first the Japanese would not believe me. Finally, they believed. They agreed not to burn our *barrios*—to be satisfied to punish only me."

"But you are alive, Tito Manuel," said Erlinda. "They did not shoot you or burn you the way they were going to burn our *barrios*. Why?"

"Yes, I am still alive. I shall never understand why." Tito Manuel spoke slowly because the wonder of his freedom was still beyond belief. "The only explanation is what Erlinda said when we started talking about the Japanese: 'The Japanese are nice people.' It was war. I was their enemy; I had fought their men. I had confessed—God forgive my lie—to causing the death of three of their soldiers. But in spite of all that, the Japanese admired courage. They were brave men themselves, you know. They said to me, 'You are a brave soldier. You obeyed orders!' They let me go free. And they did not burn our *barrios* or hurt our people."

"And ever since that day," finished Tatang, "Tito Manuel has been known as the hero of Darapidap."

"But you said you were not brave," protested Tino. "You told us how your knees shivered and your hands shook!"

"It is not being afraid that separates the coward from the hero." Tatang looked his eldest son in the eye. "It is doing what must be done, no matter how scared he is, that makes a brave man—or a brave boy."

"Oh!" was all that Tino could answer.

The children would have called for more stories, but new sounds in the treetops made them all look up. A flock of monkeys was peering down at them. The chattering seemed to be asking, "Well, what strange creatures do we have down there on the ground?"

"They remind me of the monkey we had for a pet when we lived out here," said Nanang.

"I would like a monkey for a pet," announced Pedring.

"How did you catch him?" Salvador watched the skill with which the monkeys used their four legs and their tails to swing from branch to branch. They looked hard to capture.

Then, as Nanang told how her brothers trapped and caught a young monkey, the children were sure that was the one thing they must do.

"I want a pet monkey," repeated Pedring.

"We will see what we can do," said Tino. "Come on, Salvador. There are plenty of coconuts around here. I have a knife for cutting a hole. We can make a monkey trap."

"No more Independence Day talks on patriotism or history!" Tito Manuel laughed as the children went scurrying off on their new project. "There was enough talk of our old hates and troubles anyway. This is a new day and a happy one. Let the children enjoy it."

"They do not know their way here in the forest," worried their mother. She was rolling up leftover food in banana leaves.

"No danger!" Tatang laughed as he lay down for a nap with his palm-leaf raincape for a bed and his big hat over his eyes. "We can hear those voices of theirs. So can the monkeys. There is not much chance of our having to bother with a pet monkey."

While Tito Manuel and Tatang rested, Nanang walked in silence through the forest after the children. She wanted to know exactly where they were always. And she did know, even when they suddenly realized that monkey-hunting required silence instead of shouting.

Chapter 5

MONKEY HUNTERS

Stalking quietly through the jungle with Tino in the lead, the monkey hunters found a plump green coconut lying at the foot of a tall palm tree. Any one of the children knew the familiar motions of opening a coconut, but it was Tino who had the folding jackknife in his pocket.

Neatly Tino cut a round hole at the top of the coconut.

"Is that the right size?" he asked the others.

Squinting at it wisely, they agreed it was just big enough to let in the open paw of a young monkey and just small enough to keep the closed fist of even a very young monkey from coming out. Pedring tested it with two fingers. Straight, they went in easily; bent, they stuck inside the coconut.

"What a trap!" Tino was proud of his work, as though he had thought of it himself instead of learning it from his mother.

"We should take it back up the tree," suggested Salvador. "A monkey would be more likely to see it there."

"Oh, no!" Tino tried not to let his shudders show as his eyes followed the long trunk up to the crown of palm fronds that sheltered the coconuts. "Oh, no! Climbing would make too much noise. It would scare away every monkey in this part of the jungle."

It was Erlinda, sparing Tino as usual, who had the halfway-between idea. "We can prop a tall stick against the palm tree and balance the coconut on its end, no?"

Leaning a light bamboo stick against the tree, Erlinda set the coconut on the end of it before either Salvador or Tino had time to argue. It seemed a good plan to the boys, even if it wasn't their idea.

The four children hid in a nearby clump of bamboo stalks to wait and watch. Time dragged. Small insects welcomed them with bites on bare legs, bare arms, and faces.

"We are the first good meal these bugs have had since 1945!" Salvador had been remembering his Philippine history on this Independence Day.

"That was when the Americans landed at Lingayen, no?" said Erlinda.

"And it was when our folks left these hills for good and went back to their own *barrio* to live," Tino finished. "These bugs surely are glad to see us—more glad than we are to see them."

It seemed like hours they huddled under the feathery branches of the bamboo thicket with the hungry swarms of crawling and flying insects making merry all over them. Each child was ready to say "Enough!" but not one would be first.

"I wonder why Tatang does not call us back," whispered Erlinda.

"He and Tito Manuel are having a nap," said Tino. "It is their holiday, you know. They may sleep for hours."

A new kind of bug with a super sharp stinger lighted on Salvador's neck. Just as the boy opened his mouth to say he was through with monkey trapping, there was a stir in the treetops. There was a swinging of the branches, a scattering of dried leaves, and the unmistakable chatter of monkeys.

"Sh!" Salvador's warning was not needed. The four children froze where they stood, careful not to make a sound to scare the monkeys away.

They watched the nimble animals swing into the tallest palm tree. They saw them eye the coconut on the end of its bamboo stick with curiosity. A big monkey slid down the tree trunk and sniffed at the hole, but he found it too small for his paw.

Next, a middle-sized monkey shinnied down, went

through the same inspection, and swung into another tree.

At last, a young monkey looked cautiously down the slim straight trunk. At sight of him, Pedring breathed a sharp little "Oh!" of hope. This small monkey was exactly right for a pet! If only he would stick his paw in the trap!

The monkey wound his long, strong tail firmly around a palm frond. He swung lower to get a better look at the coconut set so temptingly on the end of a pole. He swung to the palm trunk and started slowly down it. He stopped often to look about. Finally, he reached the coconut. By this time Pedring was breathing so hard that Erlinda put her hand over his mouth.

The baby monkey clung to the palm trunk with three legs and his tail. He reached one small paw into the hole in the top of the coconut. The children could imagine contentment that was almost a smile spreading over his wrinkled little face. He scraped with his claw and folded his small hand over a luscious chunk of soft white coconut meat. His mouth opened for his first bite as he tried to pull out his fistful.

The trap worked. The hole was not large enough to let out a folded paw full of coconut meat, even the paw of a very small monkey. Of course the young monkey was not going to lose good food by releasing

This small monkey was exactly right for a pet.

it. So there he clung by three legs and his long tail wondering in monkey-thinking what to do next.

"We can lower the bamboo pole," Salvador suggested. He had to admit to himself that Erlinda had a smart idea about placing the trap, better than his own.

Silently—or as silently as they could—Tino and Salvador crept from the bamboo thicket. They felt like guerrillas as they stalked soft-footed toward the monkey. What was silence to human ears, however, was noise to monkey ears.

With a chatter and a tumult in the treetops, the big monkeys were away. Awkwardly, the young monkey struggled up the coconut palm. With three legs and his strong tail he could climb, but very slowly because of the clumsy trap on his fourth paw.

"Chase him, Tino!" yelled Salvador, several paces behind his friend. "Up the tree after him before he gets away."

Tino ran toward the tree. For a minute his excitement made him forget his fear of high places. Salvador stood watching, cheering, and advising. He knew it took only one to climb the tree, and Tino was nearer.

At the foot of the tall trunk, Tino stopped suddenly.

"What is the matter?" shouted Salvador. "Go on up the tree!"

Tino was still staring up the tree when a small

whirlwind of a girl sped by him. She kicked off her wooden *bakyâ* to free the soles of her bare feet for climbing. Then Erlinda went up the tree as fast as any boy, faster than a young monkey with one foot in an unwieldy coconut trap.

Meanwhile, the monkey had wound his lumbering way to the top of that tree. He was limping along a palm frond that waved toward the highest branch of a tall acacia tree.

"I have lost him!" wailed Erlinda. "I can never swing like a monkey to the next tree."

Pedring's wails scared the monkey still higher.

It was Salvador this time who came to the rescue. He took one scornful look at his friend Valentino, who stood on the ground, his arms wrapped about the tree trunk looking helplessly up at Erlinda and the escaping monkey. Then Salvador shinnied up the acacia tree to which the monkey was trying to swing, hindered by the clumsy trap on his front paw. Thankfully, it was a strong tree with branches tough enough to hold a climbing boy.

Salvador could not have gone up much faster if he had been a monkey himself. He was high in the tree to catch the young monkey when it finally took its swing from the tall coconut tree. After a yelp of fright, the little animal snuggled trembling against Salvador. He seemed relieved not to have to worry about what to do next.

When Salvador and his armful of monkey reached the ground, everyone was too excited to mention Tino's strange behavior. By this time, Tino was himself again. He whipped out his jackknife.

"Hold him tight, Salvador," he advised as he cut the hole in the coconut trap wider.

Out came the young monkey's paw folded tight over the delicious chunk of soft white coconut meat. His little eyes skipping from one child's face to another, the monkey began to nibble at his feast. He had suffered for that mouthful! He would enjoy it, no matter what strange monsters captured him. Sitting on Salvador's shoulder while Tino held the coconut within easy reach, the monkey stuck his fist in the hole again and brought out another morsel to eat.

Pedring was standing very still, looking blissfully at the new pet. "Oh—oh—oh!" he breathed.

There was a step in the trail—their mother's. Nanang had missed no move of the monkey baiting. She led the children and their pet back to the place where Tatang and Tito Manuel were waking from their naps.

"What?" Tito Manuel rubbed his eyes when he saw the monkey riding Salvador's shoulder. "What do I see?"

"Are we dreaming, or is it real?" Tatang stood up to stretch away the stiffness from his nap on the ground.

"It's real!" sang Erlinda.

"And it's mine!" sang Pedring. "Catching it was my idea."

"Good!" Nanang laughed. "It is always good to know who owns a pet. Owners are caretakers, no?"

"Let me begin taking care of it now." Pedring held out his arms. Salvador placed the monkey gently in them.

There was much talk about the monkey. There was much experimenting with vines till one was found strong and supple enough to tether the little monkey to Pedring's shoulder. Suddenly Tatang looked at the sun and called Tito Manuel's attention to it.

"You children start down the trail toward the National Road," advised their uncle. "We should have gone farther up into the hills, but all this monkey catching took most of the afternoon. See where the sun is. It is time to start for the pass to catch the bus."

Of course the children were too polite to ask, "Which took more time, our monkey hunt or your nap?"

Down the hillside they trailed. Pedring walked in the middle of the procession with his pet firmly tethered to his shoulder. He was the proudest, happiest, weariest boy who ever climbed onto the open red bus at the pass where the National Road cut through the mountains.

Chapter 6

TATA PICOY'S STORY

The sun was low before the bus stopped where Salvador's father dozed in his red and blue *calesa* behind his small drowsy horse.

The radio, playing loud band music in the store close by, disturbed neither horse nor driver. The boy slipped into the store. He asked questions in rapid succession while his family climbed over the high wheels into the *calesa*. Pedring, monkey on shoulder, was sent into the store to call his brother, while Salvador's father joked about an extra fare for the new passenger. The children all laughed. They knew the promise of a free *calesa* ride home would stretch to include their new pet.

As they left the smooth National Road to jounce and sway over the rutted *barrio* road, the sun was a red ball crossing the line where shining opalescent sea and cloudy pink sky met. Birds were singing their evening song. Hens were settling into their roosts in the trees. Tired farmers with their carabaos were walking home at the edge of the road after a long workday.

As the horse stopped gratefully beside the home lighthouse, neighbor Gabriel was halfway down the ladder. He had kept his promise to light the lamp if they were not home before sunset.

Tita Gloria stood in their doorway with smiling Pepito in her arms. Rosario laughed and ran toward the monkey, her hands outstretched to pet it.

News travels fast in a small *barrio* where each day seems the twin of the day that went before and the day that is to follow. Word spread from child to child, from hut to hut, from Barrio Darapidap to Barrio Tomurong across the river.

"A monkey! A baby monkey!"

"Where?"

"At the house of Rodolfo Luna, the lighthouse keeper."

"Where did it come from?"

"From the mountains where our people stayed before Liberation."

"What will they do with a monkey? Eat it?"

"No, it is a pet."

"Whose pet?"

"It is the pet of Pedring."

Before the rice was cooked for supper, every child old enough to walk crowded as close as possible to the baby monkey. It was still riding Pedring's shoulder while Tino and his father searched for a piece of manila rope, strong yet light, for tying the pet to a bamboo spoke of the porch railing.

Children were not alone in crowding to see the monkey. The big boys who were already fishermen were there. So were the big girls who went to town each day to work or attend high school. Old women stopped on their way to or from the open well, whose water was so sweet, balancing their full or empty jars on their heads. Young mothers with babies on their hips came to watch. So did old men stroking their fighting roosters and young men strumming their guitars. It was still the holiday, and the *barrio* people were ready to be amused.

Even Tata Picoy, the wise old fisherman and storyteller, was there. Tata had brought the Lunas a banana leaf cornucopia full of the three-inch silvery fish he had caught in his dragnet at the river's mouth. He stayed to admire the monkey.

The older people were remembering the monkeys, who were both neighbors and food to them when they were evacuated to the mountains during War and Occupation. The very small children were seeing their first monkey. Each child had something to say.

"How wise it looks!"

"It has hands like the hands of a baby!"

"Feet also like the feet of a baby!"

"The skin of the monkey is like leather covered with hair!"

"What a long tail it has!"

"How did monkeys happen—so much like people—so much like animals?"

Tata Picoy cleared his throat. That was the signal that a story was coming. A question beginning "how" or "why" was a challenge for Old Pacifico, especially if it was a how-or-why question about an animal or something of the sea.

"You wonder why the monkey has a long tail and skin like leather?" began Tata Picoy.

"Tell us!" The villagers still stared at the monkey, but they listened to the old fisherman.

"Long, long ago, a young girl lived in a little house in the jungle. She was happy-go-lucky and carefree. Hers was not an ordinary family that must plow the rice fields or cast its net for a living. Everything she needed was given to her because her guardian was a goddess, the goddess of weaving."

The old women, and some of the young ones too, nodded their heads at mention of the goddess of weaving. This would be a good folk tale of their own branch of the Filipino people, the Ilocanos. Who in all the world could weave as well as the Ilocanos? Some of these women had looms in their nipa huts where they wove for the shops of Vigan. Others remembered homes of aunts or grandmothers where looms had gone clackety-clack for hours each day as the long strips of cloth in the familiar Ilocano designs grew in their bright reds, blues, greens, and yellows. The old women nodded. "Tell us, Pacifico." And the old man continued his story.

"The goddess of weaving did everything for the young girl. She gave her clothes, food, and servants. As the girl grew, the goddess realized she would never be a fit wife for any man unless she learned to work. Being an Ilocana, the work she should learn was the art of making cloth. So the goddess of weaving brought her a big piece of leather, a beating stick, and a basket of raw cotton fresh from the field.

"'Clean this cotton and make yourself a dress,' said the goddess to the girl who had never worked before.

"The girl stared at the cotton so full of seeds, leaves, and bits of dirt. The cleaning seemed hard. She hoped that would be all the work.

"'When I have cleaned it,' asked the girl, 'it will be ready to use, no?'

"'Oh, no!' answered the goddess of weaving. 'When it is clean, you must put it on this leather cloth and beat it with this long stick.'

"The girl sighed to think of all that hard work. She asked, 'After I have beaten it, then will it be ready to use?'

"'Oh, no!' The goddess of weaving was beginning to realize what a lazy girl she had raised. 'After you have beaten it, you must put it on a wooden spindle to twist and spin it into thread.'

"This way of getting a new dress grew worse and worse. The girl frowned and said, 'Then surely after the spinning, I will have the dress.'

"'Oh, no!' The goddess stamped her foot in disgust. 'Next you must weave it into cloth.'

"'The cloth will surely be ready to use,' said the lazy girl.

"'Oh, no!' There was despair in the voice of the goddess. 'Next you must cut the cloth in the right shape and size to make your dress.'

"The girl slumped low, exhausted at the thought of the work ahead of her. 'But that will be all. After cutting, it will be ready to wear, no?'

"'Oh, no!' The goddess of weaving felt she could bear nothing more. 'Next comes the part that takes the most time and skill. You must sew the cut cloth together to make your dress. *Then* it will be ready to wear!'

"'Oh!' The girl pouted, 'Such a hard way to make clothes—cleaning, pounding, spinning, weaving, cutting, sewing. What a lot of work just to make a dress. I would rather wear this piece of leather that you gave me to pound the cotton on. I can drape it around myself with no work at all.'

"As she spoke, the girl wrapped herself in the big strip of gray leather. This made the goddess of weaving angry. She did not try to control herself any longer.

"'You lazy girl!' she screamed. 'Take the leather for your dress if you want it. Take it for your skin also. You are as lazy as an animal. You can be an animal. Take the beating stick for your tail. It is a strong stick. It will make a strong tail. You will need a strong tail for climbing trees. From this time forth, you will live in the thick forest with only the treetops for a home. You must find your food in the jungle by your own work.'

"And that is how the first monkey came to be."

The people chuckled at Tata Picoy's story and watched the monkey sleeping like a baby in Pedring's lap.

"Rice is cooked," called Nanang from the kitchen lean-to. The good smells told that Tata Picoy's little silvery fish were ready to eat with the rice.

Her call reminded the neighbors of what they had been doing when they stopped to see the baby monkey. The old women put their water jars on their heads. Some started with empty jars toward the open well in the sand. The old men tucked their pet roosters under their arms and ambled toward the houses of their friends. The young mothers shifted their babies to the other hip and hurried home to cook supper. The big boys and the big girls walked along the road together, talking and singing. The children stood watching the monkey till they were so hungry they remembered it was time to go home.

Pedring laid the sleeping monkey gently on the split-bamboo floor beside the porch railing to which it was tethered. Then the Luna family went inside to eat boiled rice with the freshly fried silvery fish from the net of Tata Picoy.

Chapter 7

WEATHER TALK

It was hard for the Luna children, especially Pedring, to leave the new pet that first morning. They had no choice, however. First, there was the netting for *bangús* fry. Then, there was school.

Starting for school with their *buri*-palm bags over their arms, they walked backward, the better to watch the monkey. It was tethered to the porch railing again. Rosario was playing mother to it. Baby Pepito was cooing at it from the rattan hammock swung just inside the open door.

The Luna children, and Salvador also, glowed with importance that day. Again and again they told how they caught the monkey. With motions and sounds, they told how they brought it home on the hill trail, in the bus, and in the *calesa*. They described the big monkeys. They were asked over and over what they saw on the mountain where the people of Darapidap had lived during the War and Occupation.

The special attention did not bother either Erlinda or Salvador. Pedring loved it. He stood tall and held his chin high. But the questions soon bored Valentino. Other matters seemed more important to him.

"Miss Ventura," he asked his teacher, "do you have books about radios, the kind of radios that do not need to be connected with the electric power lines?"

"You mean radios that run by battery?" she asked.

"Battery. Yes, that is the word," remembered Tino.

"I am sure I can find something about them," said Miss Ventura. She glanced toward the shelves of books and pamphlets.

"If I do my lessons fast, may I read about battery radios?" asked Tino.

"I will have something ready for you," she promised.

At recess time Miss Ventura called Tino to her desk.

"Here are two pages about battery radios," she said. "This is the catalog of a big store that sells many things. They sell radios that run by electric current. They sell battery radios also for people who have no electricity in their homes. This catalog is not a science book. It does not tell how battery radios work, but it gives you a good idea what they are."

Valentino looked up from the pages to add, "And how much do they cost?"

"Oh!" Miss Ventura was worried. "Your father would not like me to give you ideas about buying one. They are very expensive. Besides, you do not need a radio here in Darapidap. You have many singers and guitars; you have the music of the waves and the songs of birds. And always there is Tata Picoy to tell stories to anyone who will stand still long enough to listen."

"Guitars cannot give us band music," said Tino. "Tata Picoy cannot give us weather forecasts so our fishermen will know when it is safe to go out to sea."

"Fishermen are good at reading weather in winds and clouds and the evening sky." Miss Ventura did not want Tino's parents complaining that the teacher from the big town gave their children fancy ideas that cost too much money. She watched Tino studying the catalog while the other boys tossed the basketball on the playground. She was glad it was Tino, rather than a boy from a poorer home. She knew Rodolfo Luna had regular monthly pay from the government as a lighthouse keeper, in addition to what he earned by fishing and what his family earned netting *bangús* fry. After a good catch, he might possibly afford a small radio, but he would not like to spend money that way.

By the time school was over that afternoon, Tino had memorized many facts about radios with batteries. He had learned catalog language that made them seem very desirable.

He found many other interesting things in the

catalog. He laughed at the machine for cutting grass in house yards. It seemed silly to Tino to have grass instead of clean-swept dirt. If anyone was so unfortunate as to have grass around his house, why not let the goats eat it? But he liked the pictures of toy trains powered by electricity, toy trucks that ran when they were wound, white machines for washing clothes, bicycles with motors, stoves that cooked with gas, water pumps with no long wooden handles, tools, and gadgets of all kinds.

When he returned the catalog to Miss Ventura's desk after school, he made the mistake of saying just what he was thinking. "I wish I lived in a city. I want machines and tools and radios like the ones in this catalog. I am tired of just lighthouses and fish nets."

Miss Ventura's answer did not seem to make sense. "You know the camachile tree?"

"Of course!" Tino walked between two rows of them on his way to school every day.

"Have you heard its story?"

"You mean how the first ones came from Spain?" asked Tino.

"They were brought from Spain, but that is not the story I meant. Have you heard the Ilocano legend of the discontented camachile tree?"

"No." Tino was not interested in camachile trees at the moment, but a boy had to listen politely when his teacher felt like telling a story.

"Once a camachile tree was unhappy because she was so plain. With plenty of sun and air, her leaves were a deep green, her branches were sturdy, and her shape was graceful. But she was sad because she had no lovely blossoms. Travelers stopped to admire the beauty of flowering vines and trees, but they never even looked up to say 'thank you' when they rested under the welcome shade of the camachile tree.

"One day she complained to the passion vine, 'How I wish I had lovely flowers like yours! How I envy you when everyone praises your beauty!'

"Now the low-growing passion vine saw its chance to climb high and see the world.

"'You can be beautiful also,' the passion vine told the camachile tree.

"'How?'

"'Let me cover you with my flowers,' offered Passion Vine.

"It seemed a good idea, so Camachile invited the vine to grow all over it, from its lowest branches to its shapely crown. For a few weeks, Camachile was content. She loved to have the cheeping sunbirds with their long curved beaks sucking nectar from the blossoms. She waved her branches in pride when travelers stopped to admire her flowers.

"But before many months had passed, Camachile found herself growing weaker and weaker. Her leaves were not so green as they used to be. She longed

for sunshine. She gasped for air. She found herself
completely covered by Passion Vine, who had never
grown so lush and strong when it crept along the
shady ground.

"'Let me breathe!' begged Camachile. 'You smother
me!'

But the vine only laughed and kept growing.

"'You invited me,' it said. 'You were not satisfied to
be a tree without flowers.'

"'I have changed my mind,' gasped Camachile.
'Leave me, and I will be content to be a plain
camachile tree growing strong and green and shapely.'

"But Passion Vine laughed again and sent out new
shoots to smother the discontented camachile tree
even more completely."

Though Tino knew what Miss Ventura meant by
her story, he could not forget the catalog, especially
the two pages about battery radios. As he went
home from school, he walked between the two rows
of camachile trees. Sturdy and beautiful, though
flowerless, they waved their green branches at him.
They seemed to be telling him, "We are just plain
camachile trees, and you are just a boy of a fishing
village, but we can both be our best selves."

The more he thought of it, the more Tino believed
that being his best self included managing in some way
to get a battery radio to Darapidap so that his *barrio*
would be more in touch with the rest of the world. He

would not tease his father to buy one. Instead, he would keep his new knowledge at the top of his thoughts, ready if there came a good chance to talk.

The first opening came late that afternoon when Tino went to the little store kept on her own porch by Conchita, wife of Gabriel, whose outboard motor was in the bamboo shed near the lighthouse. Tino's mother had sent him to buy a box of matches so that she could light the fire between the three stones in the kitchen lean-to.

With ten *centavos* in his hand, Tino waited for the attention of either Gabriel or Conchita. He thought they would never stop talking with two fishermen who were discussing the weather. The boy was too polite to interrupt.

Gabriel thought the clouds and wind said one thing. Fisherman Ramón thought they said another. Fisherman Carlos thought they meant something halfway between the rain Gabriel predicted and the calm Ramón saw coming.

"There goes Tata Picoy," said Gabriel. "Let's ask him. As usual, he is ready for any weather in his round gourd hat that sheds either rain or shine."

The old man was glad to be asked an opinion about the weather. Though he no longer went out in the *bangkas*, he had not lost his fisherman's eye for clouds, his fisherman's feel for wind, and his fisherman's nose for something in the air that told what weather was coming. Usually he could give a quick, sure guess about the weather. Today he was uncertain.

"There was a ring around the moon last night," he said. "That is a sign of Gabriel's storm." Then the old man looked up into the palm trees swaying so lightly in the breeze. He listened to the waves lapping so gently on the beach. "But there are signs of Ramón's calm also. The sea is still. It will be easy to launch the *bangkas* tonight."

"Easy to launch them," agreed Gabriel. "Launching is a small part of a night's fishing. I do not want to be seven kilometers out at sea in my narrow *bangka*, even with its steady wide outrigger, when the storm I feel in the air hits us. Look at the dragonflies flying high in the air. That is the sign of a typhoon coming."

Tata Picoy shook his head uncertainly. "I do not feel any storm coming, but I cannot be sure."

Never before had Tino spoken without being asked when four grownups were talking together. But he was full of new knowledge from his questions in town yesterday and from the catalog today. He forgot how a polite Filipino boy waits till his elders give him the nod to speak.

"What we need on Darapidap is a radio to give us reports from the government weather station," announced Tino.

The four men stared at him. So did Conchita. Even

"We need a radio to give us reports from the weather station."

Gabriel's small brown dog twitched his ears as though something unusual was happening.

"We have no electric wires coming to our *barrio*," said Carlos in a tone to finish Tino's interruption.

But Tino was not going to be turned aside.

"A battery set does not need electric wires," he said. "The weather forecast comes over the radio three times a day."

"Who could talk over the radio and tell us more about our own weather than we know ourselves?" Pacifico's sensible question satisfied the other fishermen. Though it did not satisfy Tino, the boy did not know how to answer Pacifico's question. That would be a question to ask Miss Ventura tomorrow. How could the men in the government weather stations tell the fishermen of Darapidap when it was safe to set out in their outrigger *bangkas* for the deep water where tuna fish were caught at night?

The men had nothing more to say about radios. They went back to their weather prophesying. They agreed they could judge better by eleven o'clock that night, when it was time to launch their *bangkas* to fish till dawn.

At last Conchita noticed that Tino had an errand and waited on him. Hurrying home with his box of matches, the boy was not surprised to see Erlinda running to meet him.

"Nanang needs the matches now," his sister called. "She is tired of waiting. We are all hungry. Hurry!"

Later, when the family sat down for supper, Tino could not keep still about weather forecasts and battery radios. He found that his father agreed with the men at Gabriel's store. Fishermen knew their own sea and weather. What help could they possibly get from some landlubber of a government employee way off somewhere at a city desk?

"But they get weather reports from other places. They have instruments and things." Tino wished he knew more about those "instruments and things." He would learn more at school tomorrow. Then he could argue better.

"Instruments!" Tatang grunted as he helped himself to more fish and eggplant to give taste to his mound of rice. "We have something better than instruments—our own eyes and ears and feelings. We have our own weather knowledge that we have learned from our fathers and from our years of living where the winds blow and the waves roll."

"But just tonight Gabriel and Ramón and Carlos see the same clouds and feel the same winds," protested Tino. "Gabriel says a storm is coming. Ramón says it will be a calm night. Carlos believes halfway between. Even Tata Picoy is not sure."

"Ramón is right," said Tatang. "A few minutes ago, I was on the balcony to light the beacon lamp. From there I get a better view of the clouds and sea than Gabriel gets from his porch under his papaya trees.

It will be a good night at sea. In fact, the weather is going to be so fair that I would chance taking my oldest son out with me—" Tatang looked at Tino seriously. The boy held his breath, hoping. His father repeated, "I would chance taking my eldest son out with me—if he were as old in courage as he is in years."

Tino bent his shamed head over his plate of rice. He wondered if Tatang had heard how his oldest son, who talked so big about radio, had balked yesterday at climbing a tree up which his little sister scrambled like the monkey she was chasing.

"I wonder—" Tatang pushed back his empty plate. "I wonder how much of your radio interest is in weather forecast and how much is in having something to tinker with."

Luckily, Rodolfo Luna was never stern for many minutes. Loyal Erlinda diverted him by bringing the guitar from the wall. "Please play and sing for us, Tatang."

He was still singing songs of the sea when the children unrolled their mats and stretched out for the night on the cool split-bamboo floor of the one bedroom. When he hung up his guitar, the children could hear Tatang and Nanang talking about kerosene, matches, and the little lantern to carry in case the lamp should need any care in the night.

The beacon never needed attention after he left for fishing, but Nanang was always there when he and Tito Manuel were at sea in their *bangka*. She never slept deeply. She would miss the lamp's steady glow if it flickered or grew dim.

Tino lay awake after his brother and sister were asleep. He heard other fishermen come in and discuss the weather. A few shared Gabriel's doubts, but the others were so sure of a good night that they agreed to launch their *bangkas* at the usual time. Tino saw the light of lanterns or torches as the men took their heavy tuna lines, their nets, and their outboard motors from the bamboo shed or from under the houses to carry to their outrigger *bangkas* pulled up on the beach.

Tino had fallen asleep long before the fishermen pushed out from shore for their night's search for tuna. His sleep was not so easy as usual. He was still working to improve the arguments he had given to the fishermen in the store and later to his own father. He was convinced scientific weather knowledge was more sure than the weather lore of the fishermen, but he had failed to prove it. He must find out more about it.

Tino went to sleep contentedly listening to the going-out song of the fishermen:

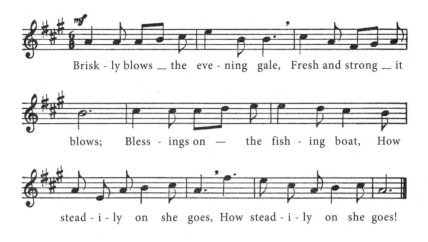

Brisk - ly blows — the eve - ning gale, Fresh and strong — it blows; Bless - ings on — the fish - ing boat, How stead - i - ly on she goes, How stead - i - ly on she goes!

He knew that in the morning he might be wakened by their coming-in song:

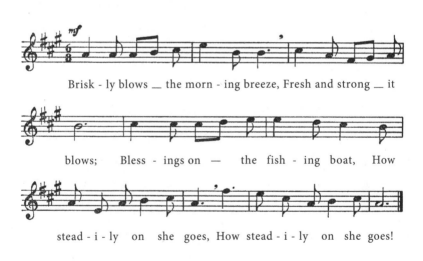

Brisk - ly blows — the morn - ing breeze, Fresh and strong — it blows; Bless - ings on — the fish - ing boat, How stead - i - ly on she goes, How stead - i - ly on she goes!

If he woke up early enough, he might even be down on the beach to sing their welcome as they chugged in with their *bangkas* loaded with heavy tuna fish.

Chapter 8

THE TYPHOON

Tino was wakened, not by fishermen's homecoming song, but by water sprinkling on his face. It was not the misty spray of showers seeping through *sawali* walls. It was the deluge of beating rain driven by wind that shook the house and whipped the thatch of cogon grass. It rattled the hooks that fastened doors and windows of woven bamboo. It bent and twisted banana, papaya, and coconut trees till they brushed the roof and pelted house and yard with green fruit. The supple bamboo branches whirled, and the sturdy camachile branches snapped.

Tino leaped from his bed mat. He saw Nanang by the light of a kerosene fire, making frantic search for things to cover the younger children—a palm-leaf cape, Ilocano gourd hats, cardboard cartons, woven cotton blankets, umbrellas. Tino spread his *buri* mat against the dripping *sawali* wall.

"What is that?" Tino's frightened whisper made no sound above the storm. He tried again, louder, "What's happening?"

"It could be—" Nanang dreaded the sound of the word. "It could be—a typhoon."

"Are the *bangkas* in?" was the first thought of the fisherman's son.

"They are still out!" Nanang's voice trembled.

"But the beacon lamp still burns!" was the second thought of the lighthouse keeper's son. Tino could see its beam through the cracks in the walls toward the lighthouse.

"Thanks be to God! The lamp still burns!" said his mother. "Lie down, Son. We can do nothing."

"I cannot lie down!" Tino paced back and forth in the shaky little house. Whenever he heard a crash, he guessed what tree had snapped or been uprooted, whose roof had lost a section of thatch, and what cart or bench from under a house had gone a-traveling. He shuddered at the frightened squealing of pigs, barking of dogs, and cackling of hens. He listened to the steady pounding of surf. He pictured waves like marching hills.

"I do not worry about us," Nanang's voice was tight and hoarse. "The posts of this house are strong. If it blows down, we are on land."

"What will happen to the fishermen?" asked Tino.

"God willing, their *bangkas* will ride the storm. They are out beyond the breakers. Their outriggers are strong and broad to steady them."

"I wish we could do something for them!" Tino shouted to make himself heard above the tumult of the typhoon.

"There are two things," Nanang answered. "We can pray for them, and we must keep the beacon light burning. It must signal 'home' to them when their *bangkas* ride the crest of the waves."

"But—" Tino hated to ask this question. "What if the light blows out or its mantles break?"

"The pressure lamp is made to withstand storms, but something might happen," said Nanang. "If the light goes out, we still have only two things to do— pray and light the lamp."

"O-o-o-oh!" Tino shivered, thinking of the dizzy height of the beacon.

"Do you know the poem in the Bible about fishermen in a storm at sea?" Nanang asked.

Tino shook his head.

"My mother taught it to me when I was a little girl. We used to say it together when my father was out in his *bangka* and the winds were blowing." Nanang's voice was calm again as she repeated the old, old poem that has comforted seagoing folk for hundreds of years.

They that go down to the sea in ships,
    that do business in great waters;
These see the works of the Lord,
    and His wonders in the deep.
For He commandeth and raiseth the stormy wind,
    which lifteth up the waves thereof.
They mount up to heaven, they go down again
        to the depths;
    their soul is melted because of trouble.
They reel to and fro, and stagger like a drunken man,
    and are at their wits' end.
Then they cry unto the Lord in their trouble,
    and He bringeth them out of their distresses.
He maketh the storm a calm,
    so that the waves thereof are still.

"I know what it means to mount up to the heavens and go down to the depths," said Tino. "That is the way it feels when a *bangka* climbs a high wave and then goes kerplop down the other side. I know how it feels to reel and stagger when a *bangka* pitches. But what about the last part of the poem? Does it mean that God will stop the waves if the fishermen cry to Him?"

"Not exactly." Nanang was thoughtful. Some things were hard to explain. "Waves roll and winds blow by the plan God made for them. Even typhoons are part of God's plan. But in His plan there is always an end to storms and typhoons. There is always blue sky and calm sea after the storm."

"Then why should fishermen cry to God in their trouble?" asked Tino.

"When they remember God, they fit into His plan," said Nanang. "They are sure the storm will blow over. They know God gives strength and courage to meet storms. When they pray, they do not panic. They keep their heads. They are brave and calm."

"I like your poem. Teach it to me, please," said Tino.

They were reciting it together when Tino's ears picked a new sound from the noisy confusion outdoors. It was a babylike whimper. Startled, Nanang and Tino looked first at the mats where Rosario and Baby Pepito were sleeping. The whimper again could be heard through the other noises. It seemed to come from the front porch. Then they remembered the baby they had brought from the mountains.

"The monkey!" exclaimed Nanang.

"We must bring him inside!" said Tino. He took a step toward the door.

"No!" Nanang stopped him. "We must not open the door on the windward side. The rains would flood us."

"But the baby monkey," pleaded Tino, listening to the plaintive whining just outside the door. "He is lonely and afraid."

"Monkeys are outdoor creatures," Nanang reminded him. "He is protected on our porch, more than he would be in the forest with this same typhoon whipping the trees. You could have him in the house, but you must not open that door toward the wind."

With a shudder Tino threw his palm-leaf raincape over his shoulder and put his bowl-shaped Ilocano hat on his head. He could go out the other door on the leeward side of the house. In the brightness of the lighthouse lamp, he could fight his way into the wind toward the monkey. It would be easy coming back with the wind pushing him. His only problem would be to grab the door as the wind rushed him by it.

"No!" Nanang guessed his plan. "You are not strong enough to walk into that wind alone."

"But hear that!" Tino and his mother listened to the crying of the monkey. "He is so young. He misses his jungle family."

Tino thought he had won when he saw Nanang throw a palm-leaf raincape over her shoulders and tie the strings of her wide, round, peaked hat under her chin. Together they could face into the storm. She hesitated, looking at her other children, tossing on their mats between sleeping and waking. Tino guessed her thoughts. Her own children should not be left alone while she went with him to save an outdoor animal from the storm.

The monkey gave one more pitiful whimper. There was a sudden gust of wind that shook the house. There was a ripping noise on the front porch as the bamboo railing splintered and blew away. The whimper raised to a thin, childlike scream that came from different places as the little monkey blew past the house. It came last from the coconut palm that grew by the front door.

Valentino opened the door toward the sea. In the rays from the lighthouse lamp, he could see a small dark object cowering in the heart of the fronds of the big palm that whipped round and round, shedding coconuts as it beat the air. When Tino's eyes grew used to peering through the curtain of driving rain, he could see the monkey clinging to the tree with all four legs and his long tail. As the tree twisted, the monkey's dangling rope twined among the palm branches, making one more grip tying the monkey to the tree. The monkey's screams subsided to a faint moan. The small creature was less terrified riding the storm in the familiar shelter of a coconut palm.

The ripping, railing, and screaming monkey had wakened Erlinda and Pedring. They wriggled from underneath the barricades Nanang had raised to shield them from the rain spraying through the walls.

"What is happening?"

"What is the noise?"

"Why does the house shake?"

"It is wet here!"

Valentino noticed how his mother tried to keep the terror from her voice while she told Erlinda and Pedring all they could understand. She did not share

with them her worries about the slender *bangkas*
far out at sea. She did not mention the lamp in the
lighthouse that must send its beam through any wind
or rain the heavens might loose. Tino felt older to
know he was bearing those worries with her.

"While you have on your raincape, Tino," said
Nanang in the voice she was struggling to keep calm,
"how about going out the front door and down the
steps to bring up the mats of cogon roofing? They are
stored under the house for mending the roof. Perhaps
we can use them inside against the walls or roof to
stop some of the leaks."

Tino was glad to do something. Venturing out the
door, he looked up. He was relieved to see the monkey
had stopped whining and moaning even though the
coconut palm whipped in frantic circles. On all fours,
Tino backed down the five steps of the bamboo ladder.
Under the house he found the wide strips of thatch.

It was not the thatch, however, that he carried up
the ladder on the first trip. It was the small black pig.

Tino explained. "He was standing to his little chin
in water under the house. You know he was tied by a
leg to a house post. He could not break free to hunt
a dry place. He was lonesome, too, and frightened.
Can he stay in the kitchen?"

Seeing the pig reminded Pedring of his new
monkey. Gently Nanang told him of the broken
porch railing. She led him to the door to see the

He carried the small pig.

monkey outlined in the glow of the lighthouse lamp. Pedring had to be persuaded that the monkey, being a monkey, was as safe there as anywhere.

Tino made his second trip under the house and brought up the cogon thatch. Then all three children helped Nanang climb on a table to fasten it as securely as possible over the leakiest spots in the roof and walls.

"It is darker!" wailed Erlinda. "The new thatch shuts out the light from the beacon. Can we have another lamp in the house?"

Tino and his mother looked at each other, panic in their eyes. They, too, had felt it suddenly grow dark, but they knew they could not blame the patches of cogon thatch. They knew the light from outside was no longer shining through the chinks around the windows or between the bamboo poles of their walls. That meant only one thing.

The worst had happened to them and to the fishermen at sea. The lamp in the lighthouse had gone out under the lashing of the storm. There was nothing to signal "home" to the fishermen of Darapidap when their *bangkas* rode the crest of the waves.

Chapter 9

THIRTY-ONE STEPS

Horror-stricken, Tino and his mother looked to each other for courage. Nanang was first to rally. "No time to lose," she said. "The lamp must be lighted right away. The fishermen need that light tonight more than ever."

Tino was already fumbling with the small wick lantern they used for night emergencies. "I will be the one to go for help," he said. "Is Tito Manuel out in the *bangka*?"

"Yes."

"I will call the father of Salvador."

"He drove his *calesa* to town late in the evening. The storm has held him there. I have not heard the horse come back, and I know he would not try it in this weather."

"Shall I go to see if Gabriel is home—or Bonifacio—or Ramón—or Carlos?" Tino's panic grew worse as his mother shook her head "no" at each name.

"That would waste our time," she said. "I was awake when the men started down to the beach. I know they are all in those *bangkas* at sea."

"Not Tata Picoy?" asked Tino.

"Not Tata Picoy," admitted Nanang. "But what could he do? How could he climb the lighthouse ladder with his stiff old legs?"

A sleepy voice from Erlinda's mat said, "Tata Picoy would stand at the bottom of the lighthouse ladder and tell the lighthouse a story."

Erlinda was too full of sleep to know tragedy was crowding them. She was drowsily amused to think of Tata Picoy and the ladder. Neither Tino nor his mother paid any attention to her half-dreaming words.

"Either you or I must go up," said Nanang. The terror-stricken face of her son told which it would be.

"I will be the one to go," she said. "We have fresh matches, still dry." Again she put on her palm-leaf raincape and wide peaked hat. She slipped the box of matches into a tight tin can and tested the dim flashlight.

"Erlinda! Pedring! Wake up!" Nanang gave her orders in a tense voice. "Erlinda, you wait in the house with the babies. Comfort them if they cry. Pedring and Valentino, stand under the house, ready to help me if I cannot manage alone. You boys hold the lantern. I will carry the flashlight. I am going out now—and up. Ask God to help me to do what must be done."

The wind swished through the house as the door opened long enough for Nanang and the two boys to slip out. Turning as they closed it, they dimly saw Erlinda sitting on her mat, yawning and rubbing sleepy eyes. The two younger ones stirred and murmured in their sleep. Baby Pepito opened one eye, stuck his thumb in his mouth, and went back to sleep with a contented sucking sound. The small black pig snored on the floor of the kitchen.

Going down the bamboo steps, mother and boys glanced at the coconut palm that whipped and twisted in the wind. In the pitch blackness, they could not find the dark spot where the monkey crouched. A soft voice greeted them from high in the tree. It was not a moan. They hoped the small monkey had accepted his high perch for riding out the storm.

"Hold the lantern high, boys. This flashlight gives poor light." Nanang tapped it, hoping to stir more of a gleam.

"The lantern flickers in the wind," complained Tino.

"Just do your best with it," said Nanang.

She was already down the porch stairs and a few blind steps across the rapidly growing puddles between hut and lighthouse. The wind grabbed her big hat and hurled it into the blackness toward the sea. Tino did his best with the lantern. He could see her leaning sideways into the wind that buffeted her. She made him think of sea gulls trying to fly against the wind. The glow from her flashlight wavered before her, casting only a faint glimmer.

If Nanang had thrown her light around in a larger circle, she would have seen that the yard was not the smooth familiar place of trampled dirt. The rain had made big puddles, deep and muddy. The wind had brought rubbish—pieces of porch railing, stiff fronds from coconut palms, a side of their neighbor's hen shelter, an uprooted papaya tree, a strip of metal roofing.

It was the trunk of the papaya tree that tripped Nanang as she fought her way toward the lighthouse ladder. The boys heard her scream. They heard the splash as she fell in a puddle. The light wavering dimly before them, they ran out to her. They tried to help her to her feet, but she crumpled in the mud.

A kerosene lamp flickered in Tita Gloria's doorway just before their own lantern blew out.

"What happened?" she called.

"My ankle!" groaned Nanang. "I cannot walk on it."

"Get the mud sled from under our house, boys!" Tita Gloria's crippled leg kept her from doing active things, but she was good at planning. "Put your mother on the sled and drag her over here. I will take care of her."

"The beacon lamp first!" Nanang was sitting up. "I can wait here. The lamp must be lighted now."

"Give me the matches, Nanang," Erlinda called through the darkness. Wide awake now, she ran down the bamboo steps and joined them. "You can hear Rosario and Pepito if they cry, Nanang. I will be the the one to climb. I have been up so many times I can feel my way in the dark."

"But the beacon lamp!" Tino shivered. "It is tricky to light. You could not do it in the bright light on a calm day, Erlinda. You can not do it in the dark and wind and rain. Neither can Pedring."

"I am so clumsy about lamps and things," sobbed Erlinda.

Then she looked squarely at her big brother. The time had come when she could not shield him any longer, but she could help him face his job. "I will go up with you, Tino. I can hold things. I will do whatever you tell me. We will go up together, no?"

"We—will—go—up—together." Tino's words sounded as stiff and frozen as he felt. "The matches, Nanang."

"Everything else you need is in the chest in the balcony of the lighthouse." His mother's forced smile encouraged him. "You can manage the beacon lamp because it is like the pressure lantern your father takes out fishing, just bigger, with three mantles instead of one. It works the same way."

"I can do it." Tino took off his hat and put it on his mother's wet hair, saying, "It would blow off anyway. Pedring, hold the lantern high. Come on, Erlinda."

So, beaming the flashlight ahead of them, Valentino and Erlinda picked their way through the wreckage in the yard. Remembering their mother's fall, they stepped carefully. The lighthouse had never seemed so far away. They stumbled over fallen branches and unknown objects. They splashed through puddles. All the time the rain beat in their faces. The wind was a many-armed giant fighting to push them toward the sea. They leaned against the wind and struggled on. Tita Gloria tried to open her door and hold high her lamp, the little hurricane lamp with a chimney to protect its burning wick. Her light sputtered and went dark. There was nothing but the faint gleam of their own weak flashlight to guide them, that and the whistling noise the wind made on the thirty-one iron rungs of the ladder that must be climbed.

Erlinda reached the lighthouse first. She had planned it that way. As she had said, she knew the ladder so well she could mount it in the dark.

"I will be the one to carry the flashlight," she offered. "I can point it up when I need it. Most of the time I can point it down so you can see your next step."

"It gives less and less light!" Tino worried. He was hesitating on the ground below the ladder. "I think it will burn out very soon."

"Then we must hurry. We must light the beacon before this flashlight dies." Erlinda's voice and light were going up—and up—and up.

Tino had never been so terrified. On the other hand, he had never faced so important a job that must be done by him alone. He gazed at the blackness of the sea. He heard the ceaseless breaking of the waves on the sand bars. He knew the strong men of the *barrio* were out beyond that surf in their narrow *bangkas*. He knew their outboard motors had no more power than wriggling *bangús* fry against the force of a sea whipped by typhoon winds.

Tino felt the rain punishing him. He felt the wind fighting him. He knew the *bangkas* were defenseless in that same wind and rain. He remembered the two things his mother had said they could do for the fishermen—pray and keep the lamp burning in the lighthouse.

Tino did the first of these mightily in his heart. He had said prayer words before—in church and at home—but this time his prayer had no words. It was nothing but a vast feeling that only God could give courage to a boy who feared high places and must climb to signal "home" to Tatang, Tito Manuel, and all the other brave fishermen. From somewhere beyond him came the strength that helped Tino up the first step of the ladder.

"Coming?" Erlinda's voice blew down to him.

"Coming!" Tino answered through chattering teeth from the second rung. Only twenty-nine more to go!

Like most hard things in life, those steps could be met and conquered one at a time. Tino was grateful that darkness blotted out the growing space below him. He was grateful for the flicker of flashlight that told where his plucky little sister was climbing ahead of him. The two were very much alone—one girl with the courage to climb any height but no sense for tricky lamps, one boy with skillful hands but a great fear of high places. They must pool their strength and forget their weakness. Together they must finish the job.

There were two things to do for the men at sea: pray and light the lamp. He sensed that women in many a hut beside the South China Sea were joining him in the first of these things. The second depended on him alone.

"Coming?" called Erlinda from the balcony beside the dark lamp.

"Coming!" called Tino from step number twenty. He had counted each rung as he mounted the narrow ladder up the side of the slim white lighthouse. Only eleven more steps to go—one at a time. His knees still shivered and shook, but he had found he could make them obey him and go up—up—up—one step after the other. "Twenty-nine—thirty—thirty-one!"

"Take my hand!" Erlinda greeted him as he hesitated. Then he took the last and hardest step from

Only eleven more steps to go—one at a time.

the top rung to the comparative safety of the balcony with its iron railing.

Tino shook the rain from his eyes. He braced himself against the wind, feet wide apart. Erlinda aimed the dim flashlight toward the lamp. Tino raised its big glass globe.

He groaned at what he saw. "I was afraid that was the trouble."

"What?" asked Erlinda.

"One mantle is shattered. The other two are full of holes."

"Are there new ones up here—or down there?"

"Nanang said everything is here in the chest!" said Tino. "I hope everything means mantles, too!"

Erlinda turned the weak glimmer of flashlight on the chest. Tino opened its top and felt in its dark hole. Erlinda knew when he breathed naturally that he had found the box of new mantles.

"Do you know how to put them in?" she asked.

"I know how to change mantles in Tatang's pressure lantern," said Tino. "Nanang says this works the same way. I hope she is right."

Erlinda was wise enough to hold the flashlight steady but ask no more questions as her brother's hands worked miracles. At last the mantles were in place. He poured kerosene in the tank and pushed the pressure pump handle in and out. Carefully he poured alcohol and watched it blaze to light the mantles. They glowed with a clean, bright light. Soon there was the steady hiss of a pressure lamp in good order. Gratefully, Tino let the glass globe down and fastened it securely in place. Then he stood looking with pride at the light that again signaled "home" to the fishermen far out on the sea that rolled so dark below him.

"Good work!" came a proud cheer from Nanang, nursing her strained ankle by the fallen papaya tree.

"Good work!" echoed Tita Gloria, standing in her doorway to hold the little hurricane lamp whose light was no longer needed.

"Good!" shouted Pedring, waving his lantern under the house. He felt he had lost out in the excitement and heroics. He resolved to learn how to care for pressure lamps before he was a week older.

Then from one bamboo and nipa hut after another came the voices of women and children, thanking Tino and Erlinda. Earlier there had been no sounds from these houses to rise above the typhoon tumult, but now that one of their fears had been conquered, people shouted from one house to another.

They talked of their concern for their fishermen. They told what the storm had done to their houses, trees, and animals. Mostly they praised the boy and girl who had climbed the ladder in the typhoon.

"Good work!" was shouted through the noisy air from all directions. "Bravo! Thank you!"

As Tino followed Erlinda down the ladder, the praise that meant the most to him was the "good work" that came from his own heart. He knew, as no one else knew, how his teeth had chattered and his legs had trembled while he climbed those thirty-one steps and did his work in spite of fear.

There was little sleep that night in *barrio* huts on the shores of the tempestuous South China Sea. Only children too young to worry slept on, turning on their mats or in their hammocks when their homes shivered in the wind or when showers of rain sprinkled through thin walls onto their faces. Children old enough to worry but too young to stay awake took cat naps between the heaviest gusts of wind and rain. Waking, they shared their mothers' anxiety about fathers, uncles, and big brothers far out in fishing *bangkas*.

Whenever Valentino's uneasy sleep was broken, he opened his eyes to see if light still came through the walls from his beacon lamp.

"Sleep, my son," Nanang said. "I am watching. I cannot sleep."

"Does your ankle hurt so much?" asked Tino.

"It pains some," she answered. "My heart hurts more. It is out at sea pounded by wind and rain and waves."

"Do you think they are safe—Tatang and Tito Manuel and the rest?" Tino knew his mother could not answer, but he had to ask.

"We can only pray," she repeated. "They have more chance because you made yourself climb that ladder to light the beacon."

Tino said nothing. The word "ladder" started his legs trembling again.

"Valentino!"

"Yes, Nanang."

"I know how hard it was for you to do it. Your father has blamed you for your fear of high places. He does not understand you because he fears nothing. I understand you. I am afraid to climb also."

"You, afraid?" Tino was astonished. "But, Nanang, you climb the lighthouse whenever the men are away and someone must go up!"

"Yes, Tino. I have never told anyone how my knees tremble. I married a lighthouse keeper. He is also a fisherman. If his wife must climb that ladder, I climb."

Tino sat up on his mat to stare at his mother in the darkness. "I thought you were brave, Nanang, like Erlinda."

"You and I are really braver than Erlinda when we climb the ladder. Like your father, she knows no fear. You and I know fear. It takes real courage to make ourselves do something when we are afraid. I am proud of you, my son."

Tino felt closer to his mother than ever before. He wanted to do something for her. At last he thought of the gift he could bring her on that stormy night.

"Nanang," he said.

"Yes, Tino."

"So long as I am with you, you will never need to climb that lighthouse again. It is my job now."

"Thank you, Valentino. I am proud and glad. Now, try to sleep. Tomorrow will be a hard day."

Chapter 10

IN THE TYPHOON'S EYE

It was dawn when Tino woke. There were sounds and smells of breakfast. There were louder noises of the typhoon still raging.

"Tatang!" called Tino.

"He is not home," said Nanang wearily. "No *bangkas* are in yet."

"Oh," was all Tino could answer. He knew it was time for the men to be home. He listened to the wind, the rain, and the waves.

"Look toward the sea. You will understand why they could not get in last night." His mother opened a *sawali* window just enough for him to peek out.

"Oh, the waves are going out instead of coming in!" exclaimed Tino. "I had forgotten that can happen in a typhoon. The wind and the waves were against our men and their motors."

"God grant their motors have power enough to hold them from blowing out to sea till the typhoon passes," said Nanang.

"But the waves will be strong then, even after the typhoon."

"Strong, yes," agreed Nanang, "but when the typhoon passes us, the wind will come from the other direction. The waves will roll toward shore again, working with our men instead of against them."

"Oh!" Tino was glad of any comfort.

There was only rice for breakfast that morning, but Tino was hungry for it—so were the other children. Even Rosario forgot how wet and uncomfortable she was when they dipped their fingers in the big plate of white rice. Baby Pepito was snug and contented, nursing at his mother's breast.

While they were eating in the darkness of their closed house, there was a sudden hush outside. The rain had stopped. The wind was not blowing. The trees were at rest. The thatched roof no longer whipped as though it would fly off the house. The songs of birds could now be heard again.

"The eye of the typhoon!" Nanang jumped to her feet so fast that her ankle twinged. "We are in the center of the typhoon. It will be still for a few minutes, perhaps for nearly an hour. Now is the time to run errands and do anything that must be done outdoors. My ankle is still bad. I will stay here with Rosario and Pepito."

"What are the errands?" asked Erlinda.

"Someone must go to the store of Conchita to buy more matches, four boxes of them. We will put them in different places to be sure that some stay dry."

"I will be the one to go for matches." Pedring was off with a paper fifty-*centavo* note in his hand.

"Next, someone must go to the house where Old Pacifico lives alone," said Nanang. "He knows everything about typhoons and *bangkas* at sea. He will tell us what the lighthouse keeper's family should do in a typhoon. I hope he can come here. If he cannot come, ask him to tell you anything we should know."

"I will be the one to go for Tata Picoy," said Erlinda. Then she looked at her big brother. "Or should I do something else instead?"

"I will do whatever Nanang asks next," said Tino stoutly.

"Anything?" asked Erlinda.

"Anything," agreed Tino.

Erlinda flashed him the smile that was so like their father's, slipped her feet into her wooden *bakyâ*, and went clopping along the muddy road.

"Next?" Tino asked his mother.

She looked him squarely in the eye. "Someone must climb the ladder. The lamp should burn today, but it must go out while someone cleans the globe and fills the tank. Someone must see how the new mantles are holding in the wind. We must be ready for anything."

"I will be the one!" Tino's words were steadier than his knees. After what Nanang had said in the dark hut last night, he was not ashamed that his knees shook. Instead, he was proud that he could say, "I will be the one to climb the ladder," and mean it.

Tino turned and hurried out into the silence of the typhoon's eye. He knew there was little time to do the work on the lamp and be down on safe ground before the buffeting might begin again.

After climbing in the dark and the storm last night, he hoped the ladder in the daylight and calm would not seem so frightful. But he found that a ladder was still a ladder and that height was still height. His legs had their old trembling, and his stomach had its old fluttering. But this time his mind was strong enough to rule. His mother had given him the secret. He was no longer ashamed of feeling afraid, so long as he acted brave. He remembered Tito Manuel's shivering knees and shaking hands when he faced the Japanese soldiers alone.

Halfway up the ladder, he heard his mother call, "Tino, when you are up there, look out to sea." She did not need to tell him what to notice from his high perch.

Three quarters up the ladder, he heard her call again, "Tino, when you are up there, look at the *barrio* and river. See how our neighbors have come through the storm."

As he stepped from ladder to balcony, he heard another voice calling. It was the babylike cry of the monkey in the tall coconut tree.

"Climb down, little monkey," called Tino.

There was a squeal and a squawk in answer. Tino saw that the rope and piece of bamboo railing had become so wound around the palm fronds that the little animal could not move more than an inch in any direction.

"Have patience, little monkey," called Tino. "Someone will help you soon." He hoped his work would last longer than the errands of either Erlinda or Pedring. Let one of the natural climbers help the monkey. After all, it was Pedring's pet. Tino had taken responsibility for climbing the lighthouse ladder, but he had made no promises about climbing trees.

Standing beside the lamp, Tino stayed as far from the balcony railing as he could. In some ways high places were more scary in the daytime. At night all things were hidden by darkness. In daylight the ground looked very far below him.

The work on the lamp was soon finished. Tino had often cleaned and filled the pressure lantern his father took fishing. His hands were nimble and skilled, even when they were shaking from the height. He had beaten the typhoon. The *barrio* was still in its calm center. There was time to look around as his mother had asked.

First, he peered out over the rolling sea, far toward the horizon. Sometimes he thought he could see a speck that might be a *bangka* riding the waves, but then it would disappear. He knew it was easy to imagine things when the waves moved, and he wanted very much to see a *bangka*. The clouds were gray and frowning, though they dropped no rain. The waves were flatter, but their great swells were high and unceasing. A *bangka* could ride them if it had kept afloat during the blow. Tino was glad his uncle was with Tatang in the boat. It was good to think there were two pairs of hands last night and now. One man could rest while the other worked rudder and motor. They would be tired—oh, so very tired.

Then, Tino looked down at the *barrio*, the beach, and the river. He pressed back against the lighthouse as he looked down, standing as far within the balcony railing as possible. He noticed what to tell his mother. The trees were alive with twittering birds, hungry for insects, seeds, or nectar. The beach was strewn with driftwood, green coconuts, shells, bottles, gasping fish, creeping shellfish, seaweed, boxes, and odds and ends of rubbish. The river was brown and ruffled, churning with big fish—sharks perhaps. They were feeding on whatever had taken refuge there. The *barrio* was alive with women and children running to their neighbors, climbing their roofs to weight down flapping thatch with heavy banana stalks, combing the beach for anything useful, fastening their doors and windows in preparation for the blow they knew would come soon.

Tino saw Pedring splashing through the deeper puddles on his way home from the store with his boxes of matches. He saw Erlinda climbing down the bamboo steps from Tata Picoy's house with the old man following her. This would be good news to tell his mother. The experienced old fisherman would give comfort with his wisdom.

Tino took the hardest step, from balcony to highest ladder rung, and began the long climb down. He reached the foot of the ladder as Pedring splashed home from one direction and Erlinda picked her way home from the other.

Their mother was at the door to greet Tata Picoy. Neighbors gathered to ask what Tino had seen from the lighthouse balcony and to hear the wisdom of Old Pacifico. They shared their problems and worries, blended in a tumult that nearly equaled the noise that the typhoon was making a few minutes ago and would be making again as soon as its eye had passed over Darapidap.

"Come with me." Tino beckoned Erlinda and Pedring aside. He pointed to the high coconut tree where the small monkey was twisted tight with his rope.

Erlinda and Pedring raced for the tree. The boy was first. With the monkeylike motions known to every

Filipino boy who likes green coconuts, he was soon up the tree struggling with his pet's rope. Pedring's hands were neither clever nor strong enough.

"Toss me your knife, Tino, to cut the rope," he called.

"I can carry the knife up to him," offered Erlinda.

Tino looked at the tall coconut palm swaying with the weight of boy and monkey. He shuddered at the long gray trunk with no notch in its bark to give toehold to a bare foot. He remembered how awkward Erlinda was with her hands—how careless Pedring was. They probably could not open the knife, to say nothing of using it.

Tino forced a smile for Erlinda. "Thanks," he said. "I will be the one to carry it up myself. I am better at untangling things than either you or Pedring."

Then, awkwardly, he shinnied up the tree. He was not as quick as Pedring. All Tino's experience in climbing coconut trees was as spectator. His grandstand had been firm ground while other boys threw down young coconuts and he thought of reasons to explain why he was earthbound. How he wished now he had climbed a palm tree at least once!

Reaching Pedring and the monkey at last, Tino hooked his shivering legs about the tree trunk and went to work with shaking hands. Untwisting and unwinding while Pedring comforted the monkey, Tino soon had the rope hanging free.

"I will be the one to carry him down," said Pedring. "He is *my* pet."

"Of course!" Tino was glad to have both hands free.

The boys were scarcely on the ground when there was a sudden gust of wind. The rains began again. Tata Picoy pointed at the choppy sea. "Soon waves will be rolling in as usual. Then waves and wind will be working *with* our men instead of *against* them. It may be hours before we see our neighbors, but now they have a good chance of making shore."

"But how can they land?" Salvador looked at the waves dashing angrily on the hard, sandy shore and rolling up into the beach grass far above the high tide line. He was glad his own father had been caught in his *calesa* in the big town instead of in a *bangka* at sea.

Tata Picoy pointed toward the river. "They will steer to the left of the beacon light. They know the mouth of the river will be open for them to land."

Tino thought of the sharks whose fins he had seen churning water at the mouth of the river, but he did not mention them. He knew it was easier to land among sharks than among mountainous breakers. Anyway, there was nothing any of them could do about either sharks in the river or waves breaking on the beach.

The wind blustered harder; the rain beat more angrily. Mothers hustled children back to their own little houses to wait out the storm. Tata Picoy climbed the bamboo steps into the *sala* of the Luna's home. It was good to have the wise old man with them when they closed the *sawali* doors and windows against the typhoon. The murky darkness within the house seemed less gloomy because he was there.

Chapter 11

THE RETURN

Tata Picoy seemed as glad to be with the Lunas as they were glad to have him share the storm with them.

"My house is lonely," he said. "It is good to be with a family when wind and rain are bold."

"It is good to have you with us," said Nanang as they settled on the floor and chairs in the dark corner of the *sala* farthest from the west outside walls. "The family of the lighthouse keeper must do the right thing in a storm. We need you to advise us."

"Let me say one thing first," began Tata Picoy, taking off his round Ilocano hat. "That Valentino of yours tried to give me and the other fishermen some good advice. We did not listen to him. We said we could get along the way we always had and the way our fathers and grandfathers had before us."

Tino sat straight. There was a new shine in his eyes. Tata Picoy talked on. "That Valentino of yours told us yesterday that we ought to have a radio in Darapidap so we could listen to weather forecasts and know when it was safe to go out in our fishing *bangkas*. Carlos, Gabriel, and Ramón ignored his idea. So did I. Those men and many others are out in that typhoon now in their *bangkas*. That is where I would be also, if I were not so old and stiff. I wonder what they think now about Tino's idea of a battery radio in our *barrio*!"

"What do *you* think, Tata Picoy?" asked Valentino.

"I think it is the best idea since outboard motors," said the old fisherman. "If the people of Darapidap start a fund to buy a radio, I will be the first one to give the first *peso*."

"Where can we keep a radio? Who will take care of it?" Tino's question sounded like an offer.

"Well, that is a question for the *barrio* council to decide," said Tata Picoy. The way he winked at Nanang over Tino's head showed that, so far as he was concerned, Tino's unspoken offer had been accepted.

As the winds shook the hut, they talked of typhoons, ships in storms, and big tuna fish. Tata Picoy described different lamps that had sent their beams from the Darapidap lighthouse during the many years since he was born in a nipa hut, standing on the very spot where his little house stood today.

As waves rolled and rain pelted, there was nothing to do within the dimness of those bamboo walls but talk and listen.

"Tell us a story, Tata Picoy," said Erlinda.

"Yes, tell us a story," echoed Tino and Pedring.

Even little Rosario lisped, "Tell—story."

"What kind of story?" Old Pacifico was always ready to tell one. His only problem was to know which one to pull from his store of true tales and folk tales.

"A how-or-why story," said Tino, "about the sea or the weather."

Tata Picoy considered. "Shall it be 'why the sky is high' or 'why crabs have strong claws' or 'why the turtle carries its house' or 'why the sea is salty' or—?"

"Tell us why the sea is salty," begged Erlinda. "I tried to drink sea water once. U-u-ugh, it was salty."

"After you hear my story, you should ask Miss Ventura to tell you why the sea is salty according to the schoolbooks," advised Tata Picoy. "I will tell you what my father told me and what his father told him and a long line of fathers before him told their sons."

The children sat on the drafty bamboo floor close to the old fisherman. Being a good storyteller, Tata Picoy waited till everyone had wriggled into a comfortable position for quiet listening. Nanang cuddled Pepito in her lap, ready to nurse him if he grew restless during the storytelling. Even with his listeners so quiet, Tata Picoy had to raise his gentle voice because of the howling of the wind, the constant downpour of the rain, and the giant waves that ran up the beach under the huts nearest the sea.

"Long ago, when the world was new, the busiest person was Ang-ngalo, the god of building. He wandered hither and yon—always working—always building. For one thing, he dug caves which he had to hide from Angin, the always-angry goddess of the wind. Whenever she found one of his caves she would blow it full of rubbish till it was not a cave anymore. Ang-ngalo, the builder, had to create trees and vines to hide his caves from the eyes of the fretful goddess of the winds.

"One day, Ang-ngalo was climbing to a cave he had carved near the top of his highest mountains. He gazed far out across the sea and saw something that made him take a long, deep breath. The ocean then was clear and pure as the tears of the sad goddesses who had made it with their weeping. It shone and glistened in the sunshine, but what Ang-ngalo saw was even more dazzlingly beautiful than the shining sea.

"Across the ocean the prettiest maiden he had ever seen beckoned to the powerful god Ang-ngalo. He did not know whether she was lonely, sick, or in danger. He knew only that, if she called him, he must hurry to meet her.

"So across the ocean with giant steps strode Ang-ngalo. Wherever one of his feet touched bottom, a great cavern gaped, making deep spots that dot the ocean's floor to this day. When he reached the beautiful maiden, she introduced herself.

"'I am Sipgnet, the goddess of the dark,' she said. 'I live in a palace that is dingy and gloomy. I hear you are the greatest of all builders. Will you make me a new palace that will be light and cheerful?'

"'Of course!' Ang-ngalo was ready to do anything for a goddess so lovely. 'Where shall I build it?'

"'Here. In this spot.'

"'What kind of palace shall I build for you, my beautiful goddess of darkness?'

"'A pure white palace,' she said. 'I am tired of things that are black and murky. I want a palace made of bricks that are white as *sampaguita* blossoms that grow in your fields and hills, white as the snow that covers the ground in cold countries far away.'

"'I know no bricks of the whiteness of *sampaguita* blossoms,' said the god of building. 'But if that is what the goddess Sipgnet wishes, that is what she shall have. White bricks will be found to create for you a great palace in this spot.'

"Then Ang-ngalo began his search for bricks as white as *sampaguita* blossoms. At last he found them. In the Kingdom of Salt, he found bricks of pure white salt.

"Ang-ngalo brought gifts to Asin, the ruler of the Kingdom of Salt. He told him of his search. He begged for enough white bricks to build a palace for Sipgnet.

"Asin was a generous and good-natured king.

"'Surely,' he said. 'You may have as many bricks as you can carry across the ocean to the spot where the goddess of darkness has ordered her palace to be built.'

"Then Ang-ngalo recruited thousands of workmen. First, they built many bamboo bridges stretching across the ocean. Then, they began to carry the bricks of salt across those bamboo bridges. Because Sipgnet wanted a big palace, many thousands of pure white bricks were needed.

"The carriers marched over the bamboo bridges day after day after day. Ocean liked peace and quiet for her waters that were so pure and sweet. She began to grow impatient. Angin, the bad-tempered goddess of the winds, saw her chance to make trouble. She fluttered over Ocean saying, 'What a nuisance is the continual procession of workmen tramping over the bamboo bridges with their burdens of salt!' Angin sympathized with Ocean about the annoying confusion made by the carriers. Soon Ocean was feeling so sorry for herself that she was ripe for Angin's suggestion.

"'Together we could put an end to this bother,' the goddess of the winds whispered to Ocean. 'I will blow while you stir up your waves. Together we can jounce and jostle the bamboo bridges till they topple over into the water with their workmen and those tiresome loads of white bricks of salt.'

"'Agreed,' said Ocean.

"So Angin blew her stormiest while Ocean tossed her waves about. Together wind and waves broke the bamboo bridges into slivers. It all happened so fast the workmen scarcely had time to scream 'Help!' before they fell with a splash into the clear pure water, dumping their *sampaguita*-white bricks of salt about them.

"And from that day to this, the sea has been salty."

The children sat silently about Tata Picoy. They enjoyed thinking of the bamboo bridges, the salt bricks, and the tricky goddess of the winds.

"Angin is surely angry today," said Erlinda.

Her words brought them back to today's typhoon and their duties as a family of the lighthouse keeper.

"What should we be doing, Tata Picoy?" asked Nanang. "We have the beacon clean and filled with kerosene. It is burning now, even though it is day. We cannot think of anything more to do."

"It is good to have the lamp lighted," praised Old Pacifico. "Even in daylight the beacon can be seen farther than the white tower. How about someone going up the lighthouse ladder to see if there is any sign of our men at sea? Have you noticed that the wind and rain are letting up a little?"

Nanang listened. She laid her sleeping baby in his rattan hammock and looked through a peephole in the *sawali* shutter.

"That is right," she said. "We were so interested in your story, we forgot our own wind and waves. It is blowing less, and the rain is more gentle."

Nanang looked at her three bigger children. "Who wants to climb the tower?"

Three voices answered as one, "I will be the one to go!" Even Rosario lisped, "I—go."

Only Baby Pepito in his rattan hammock sucked his small thumb, unconcerned.

Tata Picoy looked at the three children. "Three pairs of eyes are better than one," he said.

On went the palm-leaf raincapes again as Valentino, Erlinda, and Pedring went out together. They waded across the streams of running water toward the lighthouse. This time it was Tino who led the ascent of the ladder. He had to take a deep breath and try to stiffen his legs, but he was not ashamed of the shaking. He remembered how his mother, who seemed always so brave, shared the same fears that had plagued him all his life.

The thirty-one rungs did not seem so many as in the dark last night, nor even so many as in the calm of the typhoon's eye that morning. He counted as he conquered each one, "One—two—three—" up to "twenty-nine—thirty—thirty-one."

On the balcony the three children huddled together in the wind and rain, holding each other by the hand for comfort. Though the typhoon had moderated, the tower rose up alone to take its full fury. The children looked as far as they could, feeling like the giant Ang-ngalo gazing across the ocean.

"I do not see any beautiful maiden needing a palace as white as *sampaguita* blossoms." Erlinda was still feeling the wonder of Old Pacifico's story.

"I see something better!" shouted Tino. "At least I *hope* I do."

The others looked where he pointed. Far out, something dark rose into sight on the crest of each successive wave. They saw another dark spot—another—another.

"*Bangkas!*" shouted Pedring.

It was Erlinda who dared ask the questions that were in all their minds. "Are the *bangkas* right-side up? Are there men in them?"

Her brothers did not answer. With her they stretched their vision to see farther than their eyes had ever looked before. As the dark spots came slowly nearer, the outlines grew more distinct.

"I can see the prows of the *bangkas* rising from the water," said Tino. "They are right-side up."

"I see something more!" Erlinda squeezed her brothers' hands. "I see men in the *bangkas!*"

"You are right," said Tino. "I see someone sitting in one *bangka*—in another—in another." He was ready to shout his good news to the *barrio*.

"Nanang!" he yelled. "Tata Picoy! Tita Gloria!

Everyone! Good news! We see *bangkas*!"

Heads appeared at opening doors and windows. Women with and without raincapes and wide hats poured into the clearing about the lighthouse. They looked up at the glad faces of the three children. Then the whole *barrio* broke into an outcry of joy and relief.

"Are you sure?" Tata Picoy shouted up to the children.

"We see many *bangkas* moving this way. We see figures in the boats," Tino shouted down to him. "Their prows seem to be pointing toward the river's mouth, just as you said they would."

Then a running, shouting mob of women and children ran in all directions. Some dashed down to the beach to look out to sea. Boys scrambled up coconut trees to get the longer view. Salvador climbed the lighthouse ladder, two rungs at a time, to join his friends in their lookout. Women splashed down the puddly road, jumping flowing streams of water, toward the river's edge. Children ran to the tide line to follow the beach to the mouth of the river.

From the lighthouse tower, Tino, Erlinda, Pedring, and Salvador could watch them all—the women running in their wet skirts, Old Pacifico forgetting his stiff knees as he loped along with them, the children diverted on the beach by the treasures the typhoon had thrown ashore, the *bangkas* coming slowly nearer.

The crowd was waiting to welcome the fishermen home.

"One is red with a duck's head on the prow. That's Gabriel's *Victory*." Though Erlinda could not tell a wooden duck's head from a carabao's at that distance, she recognized Gabriel's *bangka* by its general shape and color.

"The yellow could be Vicente's *Breeze* or Ramón's *Rosita*. I cannot see whether it has blue or green trimming," said Tino.

"See the gray and white *bangka*," shouted Pedring. "Can you see something red where the motor would be? It is the *Sea Gull*, no? There are two men in it. One is big."

"That is Tito Manuel," said Erlinda.

"The other one is thin and sits very straight. That is—"

Tino and Erlinda sang with Pedring, "That is Tatang!"

"See who is coming down the road!" Salvador pointed at a muddy *calesa*, drawn by a muddier horse, careening through deep pools and brooklets in a way to make a toughened fisherman seasick. "My *tatang* has come home also."

It was hard to know whether to join the crowd on the river's edge waiting to welcome the fishermen home or stay on their high lookout, viewing beach, sea, river, and *barrio*. They stayed aloft to look and shout and laugh. They could see the *bangkas* chugging slowly toward the muddy mouth of the river. They watched the fishermen being mobbed by glad greetings of the *barrio* folk.

Salvador climbed down to hear his father's story of the typhoon inland. The Luna children were still standing on the balcony beside the beacon lamp when the dripping procession marched below them from the river. It seemed like a fiesta with everyone so gay and excited. Each drenched and weary man had his own family clinging to him. Each man was gazing at his own as though he could never see enough of the dear ones he had feared he might never meet again. The women were crying, laughing, and talking at the same time.

Even Erlinda in the lighthouse balcony was enough of a woman that her tears were mixed with her laughter when she saw her own handsome father stop in the yard and flash his smile at them.

"Tell me," he shouted so loud that anyone could hear and answer. "Tell me who saved us all by going up in the typhoon to light the beacon lamp. We thought we were lost when that light went out. We were ready to give up when it stayed dark for minutes and more minutes. Suddenly it beamed again. Then we had courage to struggle. That light has been our guide and comfort ever since. It has said 'Home. This way is home.' Tell us. Who climbed the ladder to light the lamp?"

The answering chorus was so loud it seemed to

pick Tino off his feet and float him on a cloud of happiness. "Tino! It was your son, Valentino!"

The pride on Tatang's face was something Tino would never forget. "So it was Tino who saved us!"

"He tried to save us before we pushed off from shore," said Gabriel. "If we had listened to his advice about weather forecasts over a battery radio, we might have been in our beds instead of out there whipping about like corks in an angry ocean."

"That is right," boomed Tito Manuel's big voice. Everyone listened when the *barrio* lieutenant spoke. "We must have a *barrio* meeting as soon as we are dry, fed, and rested. All the men will come together to decide what to do about the battery radio for weather signals. Valentino, you must meet with the other men."

Yelling, "I will be there!" Tino beamed down at "the other men."

"Look!" Erlinda pointed at a rainbow arching across the sky. "The sun and the rainbow are staring at each other."

"If the rainbow wins, it will rain again," Tino quoted the folk saying of the weather prophets. "If the sun wins, the storm is over."

"I think the sun is winning," said Pedring, as the three children started to climb down the ladder.

Chapter 12

THE NEW HERO OF DARAPIDAP

For days after the typhoon, the waves rolled too high for the men to launch their *bangkas*. The mouth of the river was too dangerous for netting *bangús* fry because sharks were feeding in the roily water. There was plenty of work, however, for everyone in Darapidap and in the neighboring *barrios* facing the South China Sea.

Women and children were busy walking up and down the beach, searching for treasures swept in by the storm. There was driftwood enough to keep fires burning for many a week in the stone or clay fireplaces in all the kitchen lean-tos and dooryards. Crabs, turtles, and other edible shell creatures were burrowing holes in the wet sand. Right after the storm, there were big fish the typhoon had driven ashore, stunned but breathing. There were pieces of wood of interesting shapes to suggest the toys that could be made of them—trucks, sling shots, and *sungka* boards for the shell game every Filipino loves to play.

The men and big boys were busy mending their houses. There was steady hammering as they climbed roofs to nail down loose tin over ridgepoles or to fasten a new thatch of cogon grass or nipa palm. Houses whose posts had blown crooked were straightened. Bamboo steps that had blown away were being carried home and nailed in place. Holes in walls were being mended. Unwelcome streams under houses or in yards were being channeled to run away instead of making new pools of muddy water.

The big boys and some of the women were busy cleaning yards. Fallen branches and uprooted trees had to be piled for fuel. Laundry drying racks, work tables, benches, and mud sleds had to be rescued after floating or blowing away from under many houses. Green coconuts that covered the ground must be sorted and the good ones salvaged.

Small children were busiest of all in the swimming or wading pools that had appeared everywhere. The water was brown and full of rubbish, but it was a new place to play. What fun to go wading under your own mango tree or swimming under your own house!

And of course the big girls helped the women

clean their own small houses as soon as they could fling open *sawali* doors and windows to let in the drying sunshine. Wet sleeping mats were spread on bushes to dry. Damp clothing was washed and spread on bushes, fences, drying frames, and grass. Women swept their bamboo floors with their stiffest brooms of coconut midrib in the right hand while they polished them with half a coconut shell pushed by the left foot. Rice that had been dampened in its huge storage baskets had to be spread on the ground to dry in the sunshine. At their work the women chatted together about what had happened to each family while they were separated from their neighbors by the buffeting typhoon. The women shuddered as they shared the stories their men had told about the terrible hours on the typhoon-whipped sea.

In the midst of all this activity, the *barrio* lieutenant kept his word about the meeting to discuss the plan of his nephew, Valentino Luna. The men, Tino among them, were called to the schoolhouse on the fourth evening after they were home from the sea.

"We have learned a hard lesson," Manuel said to them. "A boy told us that our *barrio* needed a radio to bring us weather signals. We thought he wanted the radio for silly programs. We knew he liked anything that had to do with machines or modern American gadgets. We paid no attention when he said the fishermen needed it for their own safety."

Tino felt uncomfortable. Tito Manuel's guess was so
nearly true. He had itched to turn the dials of a radio
and hear the wonderful sounds come through the air
from Vigan, from Dagupan City, even from faraway
Manila. The wonder of a little box that could pull
music or voices from the air waves fascinated him.
Taking care of it—cleaning and repairing it—would
be such fun. He did think about the weather reports
after he heard them at the store in the big town, but he
had been thinking about entertainment also.

Tino was wondering whether he should confess all
this to Tito Manuel and the other men. But his uncle
gave him no chance. As the *barrio* lieutenant, it was
his time to talk, and he was using it.

"Most of us are old enough to remember how we
longed for a battery radio when we were guerrilla
soldiers in the hills during War and Occupation," said
the hero of Darapidap. "We knew that some guerrillas
had radios with them in their hills. Our *bolo* men
were quick and trusty messengers, but we envied
other guerrillas with their surer and easier way of
getting news."

The men nodded. All of them could remember
those days of hardship and courage on the hills.

The father of Salvador stood up to tell something
much closer to their problem than the memories of
those old days.

"I was in the big town on the National Road," he

said, "on the night of the typhoon. Every radio was tuned to the stations that kept interrupting their programs to give weather forecasts. They talked about a typhoon called 'Patty' that was blowing our way. Everyone was surprised I had left home that evening with the typhoon coming so soon. They had been hearing about it for hours. They knew how fast it was traveling and how many kilometers an hour its winds were blowing. I thought of going back to warn you all, but I knew it was too late. By the time I could reach Darapidap, you would have gone to bed or gone to sea."

The men had questions to ask the *calesa* driver before Tito Manuel took control of the meeting again. "Now," he asked, "what shall we do about a battery radio for the fishermen of our *barrio*?"

"The cost of a radio is too much for any one of us alone," said Carlos cautiously.

"But not too much for all of us together," said Ramón.

"Here is the first *peso*." Tata Picoy reached into the pocket of his well-worn trousers.

Tito Manuel waved Old Pacifico's wadded paper *peso* where all could see. "This is the vote of the oldest and most weather-wise man among us. Will all those who vote with Tata Picoy please stand?"

Not a man stayed in his seat. As they stood, they clapped long and hard. Tino was not sure whether they were clapping for him, or Tata Picoy, or the *calesa* driver, or Tito Manuel, or for the radio they were going to buy. Anyway, Tino clapped longer and louder than anyone else. He knew he was applauding the radio.

"Now," said Tito Manuel, "how shall we buy the radio?"

"How much will it cost?" asked Gabriel.

Manuel motioned Tino to speak. "My nephew has been studying the catalogs. Perhaps he knows the price."

"In the catalog there is one that costs as little as forty *pesos*. Others cost more, even as much as three hundred *pesos*," said Tino. "Batteries and tubes wear out, so we would need money sometimes to buy new ones."

The fishermen started walking toward Tito Manuel, reaching in their pockets and opening their wallets. The *peso* of Old Pacifico was no longer alone in the hand of the *barrio* lieutenant. When the last man had given him money or the written pledge of money, Tito Manuel counted and smiled.

"Darapidap can buy a *good* battery radio, not the little one for forty *pesos*. And there will be a fund left over to take care of new batteries and tubes for a while."

There was talk among the men. They used different words, but they all meant the same. "A few *pesos* look small when you have been out in a *bangka* in a storm just because you had no warning that a typhoon called 'Patty' was headed your way."

"Now who will go to Vigan and buy the radio for us?" asked Tito Manuel. "It must be somebody who knows about radios."

"How about Valentino Luna?" asked Saturnino. "His uncle or father might go along with him."

Again every fisherman clapped. Again Tino was the most enthusiastic clapper of them all.

"There is one more thing to decide," said Manuel. "Where shall we keep this radio? In the store? In the school? In one of our homes?"

"In the house of the lighthouse keeper, no?" shouted Gabriel.

Again every fisherman clapped. Again Tino was the greatest clapper of them all. He applauded for at least ten claps after everyone else had stopped.

"Are you satisfied, or shall we put it to a vote?" asked the *barrio* lieutenant.

The voting was just as unanimous as the hand-clapping had been.

"The radio will stay in the home of the lighthouse keeper. We can plan signals to flash from the lighthouse beacon if any news comes while we are fishing." Tito Manuel was almost as excited as Tino himself. "The son of the lighthouse keeper already has learned something about battery radios. I know Tino. I can promise he will learn more. He reads and asks questions. He is a good fixer. We can trust him to keep our radio in order. He has proved that he can climb the lighthouse ladder at any time of day or night to flash signals if necessary."

There was much talk before the meeting broke up and the tired men went home to their sleep.

After Tino was in bed, there was planning and quiet laughter between his father, uncle, and mother—just too far away for him to hear what they were saying. He was asleep before Tito Manuel went home, and the house swayed gently as the parents spread their sleeping mats beside their children in the one bedroom of the bamboo and cogon hut.

A few days later, Valentino woke to a special feeling that the world was very good. The sun was shining. The trees were still. The breakers on the beach were humming pleasantly. Then he remembered the other reason he was happy.

"This is the day we go to Vigan to choose the radio, no?" he asked his mother. She was sitting on her mat nursing Baby Pepito.

"That is the plan of your father and uncle," she answered. There was something about her smile that seemed to be hiding a happy secret.

Tino jumped up and went to the pump to wash his face and hands. "We must start early," he said. "Vigan is even farther away than the pass where we went on the fourth of July."

"You have never been to Vigan," Pedring reminded him.

"But we were riding on a bus labeled VIGAN, no? And we got off before we got to that city."

"Right." Pedring was not altogether happy that his brother was going on the trip to Vigan without him, but he realized that Tino had not gone there when he was Pedring's age.

Tino was pulling on his best clothes when his mother stopped him.

"Not those clothes," she advised. "Wear the pants I patched after you wore them to school last time. Wear the blue shirt."

"Patched pants and a faded shirt?" Tino was surprised. "I should dress in my best to ride the bus to Vigan, no?"

"What makes you so sure you are going by bus?" Again Nanang had her smile that seemed to cover a secret Tino would be glad to hear. "Suppose you go to the beach and ask your father how you are going to Vigan."

Pedring and Erlinda trailed after Tino as he ran to the beach.

Tatang and Tito Manuel had pushed their outrigger *bangka* below the high-water line to launch on the incoming tide. The outboard motor shone clean and red in the stern of the *Sea Gull*. They were packing baskets of lunch and overnight clothing in the bow.

"Good morning, Tatang! Good morning, Tito Manuel!" Tino said to attract their attention.

Both men straightened and smiled at him.

"How would you like to go to Vigan by sea instead of land today?" asked Tatang. "We can stay close to shore. The water is calm at last. It seems a good day to give the first lesson in running the outboard motor to a boy who has proved himself old enough, no?"

Tino was too full of happiness to answer. He fell back on an old custom his people had learned long ago from their Spanish conquerors. He bowed low, took Tatang's rough hand in his two hands, and kissed it.

Then, because they were proud and happy for their big brother, Erlinda and Pedring kissed Tatang's hand and Tito Manuel's also.

It was Tito Manuel himself who said, "I shall be proud to go to Vigan in a *bangka* run by the new hero of Darapidap."

THE END

GLOSSARY

bakyâ [bak-YÂ]—wooden sandals

bangka [BANG-ka]—narrow wooden boat

barrio [BAHR-ryo]—village or group of houses

bangús [bah-NGOOS]—milkfish

bolo [BOH-loh]—large knife used as a tool; guerrilla warrior who carries a bolo knife

buri [BUR-ee]—palm tree with wide, fan-shaped leaves

calesa [ka-LEH-suh]—small horse-drawn carriage

carabao [ker-ih-bauw]—wide-horned water buffalo

centavo [cen-ta-vo]—money equivalent to half a U.S. penny

cogon [CO-gohn]—coarse, wild grass used to thatch roofs

fiesta [FYES-tah]—festival or celebration

garreta [gar-REH-tah]—shelter for a guard

mannikin [MAN-nih-kin]—bird common in rice fields

nanang [nah-NAHNG]—mother

nipa [NEE-pah]—palm used for thatching walls or roofs

peso [PEH-soh]—money equivalent to approximately two cents (2¢) in U.S. money

sala [SAH-lah]—living room

sampaguita [sam-pah-GEE-tah]—national flower of the Phillipines

sawali [sah-WAHL-ee]—fine bamboo strips interlaced to make wall boards, doors, and coverings for glassless window openings

sungka [SOONG-kah]—a popular game played with small shells on a board with sixteen carved holes

tata [TAH-tah]—term of respect for older men

tatang [tah-TAHNG]—father

tita [TEE-tah]—aunt

tito [TEE-toh]—uncle

ACKNOWLEDGMENTS

Thanks are due to Pelagia Galon and Consolacion Abaya, our gracious hostesses of Barrio Darapidap. They introduced their neighbors to us and helped us understand life in a typical coastal village of northern Luzon in the Philippines. Finally, they read this book in manuscript and made valued suggestions and corrections.

The folk tales are retold from *Filipino Popular Tales* of the *Memoirs of the American Folklore Society*.

The music of the "Philippine National Anthem" was composed in 1898 as the "Philippine National March" by Julian Felipe, at the request of General Aguinaldo, leader in the revolt against Spain. The Spanish words were written in 1899 by José Palma. (Only a small portion of this "National March" is printed.)

"The Fishing Boat" by Felix Borowski and Mary Howitt is from THE PROGRESSIVE MUSIC SERIES, Book Two, copyright, 1942, by Silver Burdett Company.